SAVED BY BLOOD

THE VAMPIRES' FAE #1

SADIE MOSS

For More Information:
www.SadieMossAuthor.com

1

WILLOW

"HEY! Watch it! These are my best fucking pants!"

The scruffy guy's half-lidded eyes struggled to focus on me. He scowled and wiped clumsily at the beer stain on his crotch.

I bit my lip, twisting my face into a contrite expression as I balanced the tray of drinks on my palm. "Oh my gosh, I'm so sorry, sir! That was my mistake. I didn't see you there."

"Damn right, it was your mistake," he slurred, still rubbing furiously at his pants. Then he leaned over the blonde he'd had boxed in by the corner of the bar for the past five minutes. "Don't go anywhere, baby. I'll be right back."

He groped her ass one more time before staggering off toward the bathroom.

The blonde turned to me, cracking a grateful smile as she shook her head ruefully. "Thanks for that."

"No problem." I grinned. "It looked like he wasn't getting the hint."

She sighed. "This'll teach me to go to a bar in Brooklyn

without my girls as backup. I just got through a bad breakup and thought a drink would take the edge off. Should've known better."

Her words, and the look in her eyes, struck a little too close to home. I was months away from my own bad breakup, but the feelings were still raw.

"I've been there, hon. It gets better," I said, hoping that wasn't a lie. Then I plucked a shot of whiskey off the tray I was carrying. "Here. On the house. To make up for Mr. Creepola."

She accepted the drink gratefully, downed it in one gulp like a pro, and gave my arm a gentle squeeze before slipping away through the crowd toward the door.

I headed back to the bar to grab a replacement for the shot I'd given away before delivering the drinks to a table full of trust-fund dude-bros. They all talked too loudly and were so generically handsome I wondered if they could even tell each other apart.

As I made my way back through the packed room, skirting the dance floor, a heavy hand fell on my shoulder.

"Hey! Where'd my date go? Did you fucking scare her off?"

I glanced over my shoulder at the drunk guy with shaggy brown hair. He'd dried his pants—mostly—but had somehow gotten a huge water stain on his shirt in the process. He looked like a sloppy mess.

Resisting the urge to point out that she hadn't been his date, and that *he'd* been the one to scare her off, I bit my lip. "I'm not sure where she went, sir. I had to deliver drinks. Sorry."

I turned away, but he caught my shoulder again, spinning me around. He invaded my personal space, pressing up against me. "Well, since it's your fault I struck out, the least you can do is make it up to me. I don't usually go for brunettes, but what the hell. I'll make an exception for you."

His hands latched onto my hips as his beer breath wafted into my face. I grimaced, wriggling out of his grasp and holding the empty tray in front of me like a shield.

"Sorry. I'm working. And we're not allowed to fraternize with customers."

With that weak excuse, I darted away into the crowd, heading back toward the bar. The bartenders on duty tonight were both burly guys, which I hoped would dissuade Mr. Creepola from following me.

My friend Grace, another cocktail waitress at Osiris, would've handed that guy his ass for talking to her like that. I wasn't quite bold enough to do more than give a firm "no," but for a girl from Ohio who'd only been in New York for eight months, I thought I was doing okay.

Unfortunately, this particular creep was persistent as hell. He didn't follow me to the bar, but every time I ventured out to deliver drinks, he tagged along after me, leering at my breasts and making really bad sex puns. His name was John or Tom or something, and he smelled like sour milk and disappointment. I wanted to whack him upside the head with my tray, but I really couldn't afford to lose this job. So I tried to ignore him. Just another Saturday night in New York, right?

By the time last call rolled around, John or Tom was beyond drunk. He lingered by the door, licking his lips and staring at me until the lights went on and the last few patrons stumbled out.

Finally.

I was happy to have rescued the hapless blonde girl, but I should've seen this coming. Jerks seemed drawn to me like magpies to pieces of tinfoil.

Wanting to give Mr. Creepola plenty of time to stagger home, I offered to finish cleaning up. The bartenders happily took me up on it, slipping out to meet up with friends or resume drinking somewhere else.

Shaking my head in bemusement, I started stacking the mats so I could mop behind the bar. Their partying stamina made me feel old, and I was way too young to feel that way.

It was after 5 a.m. when I finally left work. I took a deep breath as I stepped out of the bar, glancing down the street to make sure Tom—I'd made an executive decision that was his name—was gone. Sadly, jerks like him weren't hard to come by in the city. It'd taken me months to adjust to the gauntlet of walking New York's streets. At least once a day, I was catcalled by some guy who thought the way to a woman's heart was yelling about her ass as she got on the subway.

That was one thing I missed about Ohio. People weren't quite so openly disgusting. They kept their gross thoughts to themselves most of the time.

I checked my phone. Five fifteen.

Ugh. Damn you, Tom! By the time I get home it'll be almost time to get up again.

Giving a sharp tug on the handle, I made sure the bar was firmly locked behind me. The neighborhood was quiet now, the streets mostly empty. Even the big city slowed down a little at this hour.

I decided against taking a cab back to my place—that was thirty bucks or more that could be put toward something better. I was pinching every penny right now, trying to not just make ends meet but to save up for my future.

Besides, I'd walked home by myself plenty of times now. I'd

probably get home faster on foot than I would if I had to wait around for a cab.

As the cool breeze ruffled my hair, I tried to let the crappy night roll off me.

It doesn't matter. Don't let it get to you.

My job at the bar was just something to tide me over and help pay the rent. My real passion wasn't serving drinks to drunk patrons and smiling sweetly as lecherous men stared at my chest. I loved to bake more than anything else.

Working at Carly's Confections, an adorable little family-owned shop in Flatbush, fed my soul in a way cocktail waitressing never could. And one day—maybe not one day soon, but *one day*—I'd own my own bakery.

That was a dream I'd only recently started to speak out loud. For years, I'd felt silly even thinking it.

But it could happen, if I wanted it bad enough and worked my ass off for it. I'd already proved to myself that I was brave enough to make drastic changes in my life—leaving Kyle and moving to New York had been one of the hardest things I'd ever done, but it had absolutely been the right choice.

My steps lightened at the thought. I wasn't "Willow Pearson, sad housewife" anymore. I was "Willow Tate, badass rescuer of blondes in bars." And I was only twenty-seven. There was still plenty of time for me to build an amazing life.

A gust of chilly wind pushed at me from behind, raising goose bumps along my exposed skin. I wrapped my arms around myself and picked up the pace, wishing I'd remembered to bring a jacket. Spring was on its way, but the nights were still cool.

Some of the other cocktail waitresses wore skin-tight dresses that shoved their boobs practically up to their chins and showed off so much leg they couldn't bend over without flashing the room. They definitely made better tips than me, but I couldn't quite work up the guts to mirror their fashion choices. My silky purple tank top and dark skinny jeans were as sexy as my work outfit usually got, and I still somehow ended up with creeps like Tom hitting on me aggressively.

Grace had been trying to get me to expand my work wardrobe for a while. Her philosophy on dating was that you had to date some frogs to find the prince, so you might as well get through the frogs as quickly as possible. I'd been lying when I told Tom we couldn't fraternize with customers—no such rule existed.

And Grace fraternized the hell out of them.

She regaled me often with stories of her hot or disappointing one-night stands with bar patrons. When I told her I hadn't had sex with anyone since my divorce went through eight months ago, her jaw had practically hit the floor. She was dead set on getting me "back on the horse," as she put it, and couldn't seem to comprehend how I'd managed to live without sex for eight months.

I didn't tell her it'd actually been more like *twelve* months since my last sexual encounter.

Or that it'd been nine years of quick, bland sex before that.

I don't think I could handle seeing the pity in her eyes.

Another gust of wind hit me, colder than the first, and I gasped, my teeth chattering. I'd gotten so lost in my thoughts, I'd stopped paying attention to my surroundings, but the biting wind made me wish I were home already.

Suddenly, the dog barking in the distance stopped, and a new sound filtered into my ears. Footsteps. Light and quick. Nearby.

The hairs on the back of my neck stood up.

Oh shit. That can't be Tom the Creep, can it? Maybe he was more patient than I thought.

I picked up my pace. I'd walked this route dozens of times at night, enjoying the quiet neighborhood streets illuminated by intermittent pools of light. It was the only time this huge city, usually so full of hustle and bustle, felt peaceful.

But it didn't feel peaceful right now.

The footsteps came faster, matching my pace. They came from behind me, along with a low sound that could've been clothes rustling, or maybe someone breathing.

My heartbeat sped up, blood rushing in my ears.

Maybe walking home alone hadn't been a great idea after all. I'd gotten too comfortable with the empty streets and the illusion of safety. But there were bad people everywhere. I should never have forgotten that.

Calm down, Willow. Maybe it's nothing. Just some jogger out for an early morning run or something.

Breathing fast, I darted a glance behind me.

There was nothing there.

I stopped, sweeping the entire street with my gaze.

Nothing.

My body tingled as unspent adrenaline coursed through my system. I let out a shaky laugh, pressing a hand to my chest. I hadn't freaked myself out this bad since my first couple of days in New York, when I'd been convinced danger lurked around every corner.

"Jesus, Willow. Get a grip."

I resumed walking, but I'd only made it a few steps when a new sound came from behind me.

A low, breathy hiss.

I whipped around so fast the ends of my ponytail stung my skin. "Who's there? I'm not—"

The words died on my lips.

A chill ran through my veins.

What emerged on the street behind me wasn't Tom or John or whatever his name was from the bar. Fuck, I wished it had been.

Because this was so much worse.

2

WILLOW

OUT OF THE shadowy mouth of an alley rose a monster almost twice my size. It was made of smoke and shadows, so dark it was almost impossible to judge its true shape. For a moment, my mind balked at what I was seeing, refusing to process it as an actual creature.

It's not real. It's just a shadow being cast by... by... nothing. Or a trick of the light! Or I'm so tired I'm hallucinating.

While my thoughts chased themselves in circles, the shadow creature stood still and silent, watching me. I couldn't quite make out its face. Every time I thought I saw some hint of its features, the light shifted, swallowing them back up in darkness.

I swallowed, frozen in place.

I'd always been a planner and worrier, prone to playing out disaster situations in my head. I'd imagined what I'd do if someone tried to mug me, if I was attacked by a rapist, or if I got trapped on the subway. I'd planned for those situations as best as I could.

But I had never, in all my life, planned for something like this.

My blood felt like ice water, thin and cold. I tried to breathe, but my chest seemed locked, unable to accommodate air.

This isn't real. It can't be.

Time seemed to hang suspended as the creature and I stared at each other. I felt trapped in this moment, unable to break free. Some part of my brain screamed at me to run, while the part that actually controlled my muscles shut down like a dying machine.

Then the shadow creature lurched forward, swiping out with a massive, claw-tipped hand.

On instinct, I ducked, stumbling backward several feet.

The movement shocked my body back to life. I regained my footing and turned, sprinting away. My chest burned as my fists pumped, my feet hitting the pavement with sharp slapping noises.

I barely paid attention to where I was running, only vaguely aware that I needed to go south and west to reach my apartment.

It was impossible to hear anything over the sound of my breaths and the blood rushing in my ears, and I didn't dare look back to see if the monster was behind me. I had no plan, no strategy, except to get as far away from that indescribable horror as I could.

When I careened around a corner onto a side street, I almost tripped on the curb. It was darker here, the street lamps spaced farther apart. But it was too late to choose another route. I dashed forward, pain stabbing my lungs.

I almost didn't see the shadow creature until it was too late.

It seemed to rise up out of the ground in front of me, its large, broad form blocking my path.

My feet scrabbled on the pavement as I skidded to a stop, staring up at the thing in shock. It'd been behind me, hadn't it? How the hell had it moved so fast?

The shadowy figure reached for me, its long arms snapping out like whips. When its cold fingers brushed my shoulders, panic blazed through my body, lighting me up from within. Instead of curling up into a ball or running hopelessly, I lunged forward with a primal shriek. Despite its shadowy appearance, the thing was corporeal. When I landed my first blow, I realized it was as solid as I was.

I fought like a berserker, striking over and over again in a flurry of fists and limbs. Fear and a desperate will to live urged me on, even as the strength in my muscles waned.

But it wasn't enough.

My initial blows seemed to have caught the creature off-guard, but it recovered quickly. Its cold hands grabbed hold of me, and I belted out a scream.

No one heard. No sirens sounded in the distance.

No one ran to help me.

The shadow creature was strong, much stronger than me. The rough skin of its palms and fingers sent a shiver down my spine as it clamped its hands around me like twin vises. It was impossible to wriggle free.

No. No, please, no!

Letting its grip support my upper body, I swung my legs up, kicking out hard with both feet. They connected with the creature's midsection, and it let out a breathy grunt, dropping me.

I landed on my back with a thud. All the air left my lungs, and I sucked in tiny, gasping breaths as I rolled over onto my stomach. I pulled myself away on my elbows, fear rising like an ocean wave inside me, threatening to drag me under.

My lungs finally stopped seizing. With a desperate sob, I started to rise, half-crawling as I scrambled forward.

I didn't know where to go. My apartment was still blocks away. And why would I be any safer there? Real nightmares, the ones that had form and substance like this one, didn't disappear when you hid your head under the covers.

Before I could regain my feet, a massive fist struck me from behind. I collapsed on the sidewalk, smacking the side of my face on the pavement. Pain radiated through my cheek and across my back.

I groaned and rolled over, scooting awkwardly backward on my butt. My vision blurred as my head pounded. When the thing got near, I kicked out again. But I was losing strength and coordination. It caught my foot, twisting sharply.

An agonized scream burst from my lips as something snapped. My breath came in sharp gasps, burning my lungs like fire. The shadow creature pulled, sending a fresh wave of pain through me as it dragged me over the rough sidewalk toward where it crouched.

It loomed over me, its shadowy face blocking out the street lamps above us. For just a moment, I thought I saw the features of a man behind the dark mask—then I blinked, and they disappeared.

"Wait! Please, don't do this! Somebody help me!"

My voice was unrecognizable, thin and desperate. I could barely breathe, but I kept screaming for the thing to stop, for someone to come.

Saving the blonde from Mr. Creepola at the bar felt like a lifetime ago now, even though it had only been a few hours.

God, I wished I could go back.

Back to when I felt like I could handle what life threw at me. Before everything I thought I knew about the world was turned on its head.

Back to a time when I wasn't about to die.

The shadow creature's weight bore down on me, pinning me to the ground. It leaned closer, invading all my senses. The whisper of its breathing filled my ears as puffs of cool, fetid air hit my face. Its large form cast a shadow over me, seeming to devour all the light around us.

One cold, sharp claw ran down the side of my face. Then its other hand slashed down my body.

Agony enveloped me.

I screamed again, though my throat was already sore and raw. The pain was like nothing I'd ever felt before. Overwhelming and agonizing. Shock stole the last of my strength. My head hit the ground with a hard thump, but I barely felt it. My body arched against the weight of the shadow creature holding me down, as if my atoms were trying to tear themselves apart to escape.

Through bleary eyes, I caught the glint of a blade as the shadow creature raised it high.

What the hell does it need that for? It's got... fucking claws.

The last incoherent thought flew from my mind as the knife bit into my skin. My body had been through too much. It couldn't process any more pain, any more fear. My heartbeat slowed, and my eyes rolled back in my head.

I wasn't even scared anymore.

Just tired.

So tired.

3

JERRETT

WE'D BEEN STALKING the creature for almost a week now.

Without fail, every night the three of us—Sol, Malcolm, and I—were hot on its heels. But every time we got fucking close, it would escape our grasp. It was fast, almost vampire fast, and smart.

I lashed out in frustration, slamming my fist into the side of a building as we passed. The brick crumbled under the force of the blow, leaving a gaping chunk missing from the wall.

"Enough with the property damage, Jerrett," Malcolm growled. The neon lights from a nearby bar made his dark brown hair glow purple. "I'm as frustrated as you are, but that's not helping."

"Yeah? I beg to differ. I found it extremely helpful." Smirking, I shook out my hand. Fragments of brick and dust fell to the ground, but I did feel a little better.

"That shade can't be allowed to roam the streets like this. Someone is going to get killed. Or worse." Mal's expression was hard.

"Is it just my imagination, or is it getting stronger too?"

"Not your imagination," Sol confirmed.

Every time we encountered the shade, it had grown in size and power. It was smart too. It knew when to fight and when to retreat. And being cornered by three vampires seemed to be its ideal retreat time. As fucking flattered as I was, it was a royal pain in the ass to watch it slip through our fingers again and again. We couldn't let this continue.

Sol moved ahead of me through the shadows.

"Do you smell something?" I whispered.

He nodded, his eyes drifting closed as he sampled the night air.

My youngest brother had been on the brink of death before I'd turned him all those years ago. It'd been too late to save his sight, but not too late to save his life.

We hadn't been born as brothers, the three of us, but we'd been through so much together it was what we had become. What was the expression humans used? *Blood is thicker than water.*

The three of us had spilled enough blood together that our bond could never be broken. I'd lived over two thousand years now, and these two men were the only people I trusted with my life. We fought together, we drank together, and we hunted together.

Sol sniffed the air again, his nose wrinkling thoughtfully.

Blind or not, he was one of the best hunters I'd ever met. His other senses, heightened by vampire power, more than made up for his lack of sight. He also had a strange connection to the world most vampires didn't have—a sixth sense that allowed him to sense auras and feel out his surroundings. A human passing him on the street would likely never even know he was blind.

"It's nearby." His eyes flew open, the green of his irises

framing pure white pupils. "And it's not alone. I smell something else too. Human. Female, I think."

"Goddamnit. Let's go!"

I urged him forward, following close behind. The three of us shadow ran through the quiet streets, moving as silently as ghosts.

This wasn't supposed to be our fucking job, of course. The responsibility had fallen to us because the vampire king of North America, the one who was supposed to be our leader, didn't feel like taking the reins. Instead, he spent his days indulging in pleasures of the flesh and feasting on fresh blood.

No one had more disdain for King Carrick than Malcolm, but Sol and I came close. Once upon a time, vampires had actually been the leaders of all supernaturals. The vampire court had settled disputes between other races, kept supernaturals safe, and made sure humans remained in the dark about our existence.

Carrick's reign wasn't about any of that. His power benefited him, and it benefited the sycophants who threw themselves at his feet. But he didn't seem to care much about what happened outside the Penumbra, the shadowy swath of land where his court resided. If we waited for the king to do anything about it, there'd be thousands of rogue supernaturals roaming the streets of New York, taking their pick of the humans on offer.

This particular monster was proving to be a bit more difficult than we'd anticipated. It had strength and speed that nearly matched ours, making it a formidable opponent.

I snorted under my breath as I raced down the street after Sol.

That's all right. I like a challenge.

The long hunt would make it all the more satisfying when we finally took the beast down.

And if I had my way, that would happen soon.

"I smell blood," I murmured, slowing slightly. "Sol? What do you sense?"

The scent tickled my nostrils as concern made my muscles tense. The blood was fresh and sweet. This wasn't some poor animal who had been hit by a car and was half decomposed already. It was the human Sol had sensed, and judging by the strength of the scent, she was bleeding out.

I'd bet my last fucking bottle of Glenfiddich the shade had attacked her, but even if I was wrong, she still needed our help. Whoever this girl was, she didn't have long.

I took the lead, and the three of us darted toward the next street. When we rounded the corner, I skidded to a stop.

The undead creature of darkness crouched low over a body, its long fingers wielding a pointed blade. My eyes took that in at a glance, but what arrested my movement was the sight of the woman. She lay sprawled on the ground as the shade carved sick patterns into her beautiful skin.

Malcolm spoke before I did, giving voice to my thoughts. "It's… her."

He was right.

I recognized this woman—and I was sure my brothers did too.

I'd seen her during our last few hunts. I mean, fuck, I'd seen a lot of people—but I'd *noticed* her. She kept popping up in our path, and her innocent beauty had been a pleasant distraction from our tireless search for the shade. A few nights ago, we'd passed by her as she cut through a park several blocks from here.

She was rather tall, with a slim build and soft curves that filled out her clothes perfectly. Her hair was a deep brown, bordering on black, and her eyes lit up when she smiled. She hadn't smiled at us, of course. We'd been hidden in shadows, removed from human sight. But as she walked by, I'd felt the strangest urge to step into her path and bask in the radiance of her light.

Sol hadn't shut up about how fucking good she smelled, and though his senses were much sharper than mine, I didn't need him to tell me that. Mal was too fucking stoic to say anything, but I knew she'd caught his eye too. How could she not be?

We'd all seen hundreds of stunning women over the years, especially before we left the king's court. Carrick had an eye for beauty, I'd give the old king that.

But this woman put them all to shame. She was beautiful, yes, but it was something more than that. Her scent was intoxicating, rich and sweet with a note of something earthy I couldn't quite place. There was an innocence and earnestness about her that drew me in—made me ache to ruin that innocence at the same time I wanted to protect it at all costs from the harsh world.

She was entrancing. Mesmerizing.

And she'll be dead in a minute if we don't act quick.

The creature hadn't noticed us, its focus entirely on the strange patterns it was carving into the woman's skin. My lips curled back in rage, but the shade's distraction would serve us well. Now was our chance to destroy it.

I glanced over, meeting Malcolm's gaze. His eyes narrowed angrily, a line cutting between his thick brows. He hated to see the blood of an innocent spilled. The fact that she was so magnetic only made it more of a tragedy. We had to save her. And if we were too late, at least the monster would suffer for what it had done to this girl.

I squeezed Sol's shoulder, and he nodded sharply. He already knew what the plan was. We'd danced to this song of violence hundreds of times before.

"Now!"

At my call, we streaked forward like lightning, throwing ourselves at the shade. Mal and Sol tore it away from the girl, and I landed a blow that sent it flying backward.

The shade bellowed a breathy cry as it flew through the air. Its blade clattered to the pavement. The creature righted itself, hunching low like a wild animal about to strike. Then, without warning, it darted away and crawled up the side of a tall building, vanishing over the rooftop.

"Fucking coward!"

I sprinted toward the building, then stopped. My predator instincts urged me to give chase, to hunt the fucking thing down and kill it—slowly and painfully. But another instinct, one I didn't quite understand, froze me in place.

"Damn it. She's dying. Malcolm?" Sol's voice was tense.

My jaw clenched, and I pushed my hair out of my eyes as I stared up at the dark roof, waiting for Mal's response.

We had a choice, and we needed to make it quick. We could scale the building and follow the shade, and this time we'd probably catch it. This was the closest we'd gotten in days.

We could do that...

Or we could try to save the girl.

As my feet turned and led me away from the hunt, back toward the beautiful, blood-streaked woman lying like a broken angel on the sidewalk, I realized it wasn't a choice at all.

Mal didn't say anything, but he dropped to his knees in front of her.

And that was answer enough.

4

MALCOLM

She was dying.

I'd seen the spark of life leave more humans than I cared to remember, and I knew what it looked like. What it smelled like.

The shade had cut deep. There was so much blood on the ground the woman looked like she was floating in a dark pool. Her fair skin was painted red, rivulets pulsing from the bizarre patterns carved into her flesh.

My fangs dropped as I leaned over her, the tangy aroma of her blood invading my senses. She smelled delicious, like cherry and almond. If I were less disciplined, I would latch onto her wounds and drink until there wasn't a drop of her sweet blood left.

But I was not that man.

I inhaled sharply, wrestling with my self-control. This was the closest I'd come to breaking my vows since I had made them all those years ago.

I had made two promises to myself. The first was never again to drink blood from a human. There had been enough pain and suffering caused by our kind over the years. I wasn't going to add to it anymore.

Draining an innocent human just to satisfy my hunger for a time was too high a price to pay. The guilt that lingered was worse than the cravings for blood ever could be. And there were other ways to survive—less pleasant, but less barbaric.

"She's dying." Sol's sightless eyes were wide as his fingers ran lightly over her slick skin, feeling her pulse. "She's lost too much blood. Her heart is failing. She has five minutes, maybe less."

"Fuck." Jerrett stood over us, his feet shifting restlessly as he stared down at her. "Fuck!"

She smelled so intoxicating. Was it because I'd gone so long without drinking fresh human blood, or was hers particularly seductive?

I suppose it's only right that the most beautiful woman I've ever seen has the most tempting blood.

My mind buzzed. My brothers were looking to me for an answer, but my brain felt sluggish, as if I were drugged. All I could focus on was the girl.

The second vow I'd made had been to never turn another human. No one deserved the life the three of us had been cursed to live. I refused to spread our disease like it was a gift as some vampires did.

"Mal!"

Jerrett dropped to one knee beside me. The piercings in his lip and eyebrow glinted in the dim light as he locked eyes with me. His usual smirk was gone, replaced by a grim, desperate expression I'd never seen before.

"I know." My nostrils flared, and I clenched my jaw. A war raged in my heart. "I *know*, Goddamnit."

"She's almost out of time," Sol said softly. He didn't wear his emotions on his sleeve like Jerrett did, but I could hear the intensity in his voice.

The unspoken meaning of his words made my stomach churn. They were waiting for *me* to decide. I could sense my brothers' bodies vibrating with tension. They were desperate to save this girl, but out of respect for me, they held back. They knew how I felt about spreading our cursed condition. I'd taken an oath never to do it again, and I had meant to keep that vow forever.

This is a fucking mistake.

The cool, rational part of my brain made one last attempt to warn me, but its voice was soft and feeble.

I couldn't just let this girl die. A woman as vibrant and full of life as this must be loved by many people. They would be heartbroken to lose her.

They'll lose her anyway if you turn her. You know that.

Gritting my teeth, I silenced the voice whispering in my head. In truth, I wanted to be selfish. Though I didn't know her, I felt strangely attached to her. Every glimpse of her over the past week was etched into my memory. The way she'd absently brushed her long, dark hair over her shoulder. The long line of her neck as she looked up into the night sky and sighed.

I wanted to know what she'd been thinking to make her sigh like that. It broke my heart to think I might never find out.

"We save her."

The words dropped like lead weights from my tongue, but my heart lightened immediately. The torment of indecision was over. I had made my choice.

My brothers nodded, relief clear on their faces. Sol's green eyes that saw nothing and everything burned into me, and I could almost feel him reading my thoughts.

“There’s no other way, Malcolm,” he murmured.

I knew he was right. There was only one thing that could save her now. Even if we could get her to a hospital in time, no doctor could save her when she was this close to death; the time for human intervention was long past. The shade had done too much damage, carving patterns deep into her skin.

My jaw clenched at the sight of her cruel wounds. I promised myself we would catch the undead monster and make it suffer.

But that was a task for another night.

Right now, I would be the one to suffer. It was the only way.

I pulled up my sleeve and bit down hard on my wrist, barely flinching at the piercing pain of the puncture wounds. It hurt, but I was used to the sting. All vampires grew accustomed to it. And in the right context, the pain could easily edge over into pleasure.

Shoving those thoughts away, I kept my eyes focused on the woman.

I gently lifted up her head. Though she still showed some signs of life, her light was fading away. Her face slackened. Her chest rose and fell quickly as her breathing became more erratic. She was struggling now, her body giving up on itself. Sol’s estimate of five minutes had been generous. She was slipping over, hovering in the space between life and death.

My blood was her last hope.

I held my wrist to her mouth. For a moment, she didn’t respond.

“Come on. Come on, damn it.” Jerrett stared at her face as though he could bring her back to life by force of will alone.

I adjusted my grip on her neck, pressing my bleeding wrist harder to her lips. Would it fail? Had I hesitated too long? It’d been a long time since I’d witnessed a transformation. I’d seen ones performed on dying humans before, but never ones this close to death. Perhaps I was too late.

Sol hummed low in his throat, and I heard him mutter a prayer to Fate.

At last, the girl's eyelids fluttered open. Her pupils were blown out, making her hazel eyes appear almost black. She looked up wildly. I wasn't sure she even registered our faces, but she latched onto my wrist, an instinctual reaction.

Her lips closed around my skin, and her throat moved as she drank greedily. Color began to return to her cheeks, the ashen palor fading from her bloodstained skin. She really was exquisite.

"It's working," I said quietly, trying to hide the naked relief in my voice.

I supported her neck as she drank her fill. It'd been over four hundred years since I was turned, but I still remembered how it felt. Immortality and power had flooded my system—a high like nothing else a human could experience.

The pain would come later, as the body completed the change. But the moment of transformation was pure ecstasy.

I also hadn't fed a human in hundreds of years, so perhaps my memory was fuzzy. But this felt different. More intense, somehow. As she drew the blood from my body in deep pulls, something shifted between us. It was a connection formed of pure, shared pleasure.

Slowly, the cuts the shade had gouged into her body began to close. She sat up, cupping my wrist in her hands as she continued to lap at me. I let out a low grunt and tightened my grip around the back of her neck, trying to keep myself grounded as desire flooded me.

God, I hope she won't hold it against me that I saved her life. That I gave her this curse.

The girl was coming back to herself now. Her eyes cleared, the mesmerizing hazel returning. The sight was so beautiful it called a smile to my face. I let out a huff of relieved laughter, and she tilted her head, looking up at me in surprise. We were both high from the change, lost in each other.

In that moment, I lost control.

Without thinking, I leaned down to kiss her.

If I can't taste her blood, I'll taste those pretty lips.

Her mouth was warm and pliant, wet with my blood, and she let out a slight moan as I flicked my tongue out to lick away a drop. She kissed like she was discovering the world through our connection, like she'd been waiting for this kiss her whole life.

I pulled back slowly, breathing deeply as I regained my senses.

Then she moaned again, but not in pleasure.

"What the fuck?" Jerrett leaned forward, tensing.

The girl's body jerked as the color drained from her face once more. She fell back, and I only barely managed to stop her head from hitting the ground. Her eyes rolled back in her head, and to my horror, her wounds reopened.

"What's happening?" Jerrett's voice cut through the dark night. "She's getting worse!"

"The wounds are reopening. Why?" Sol asked.

I didn't respond, because I had no answer.

Goddamnit. This had never happened before. It wasn't how it was supposed to work. Never in four hundred years had I heard of a failed transformation. It just didn't happen—unless the person was already dead.

"What do we do?" Jerrett paced to her other side, dropping to his knees.

"I don't… I don't know."

"Let me try," Sol said grimly.

He pushed me out of the way and bit his own wrist until it bled. He let the blood drip onto her full lips like candle wax. Her body stopped seizing, and she sat up, gripping his arm like she had mine. A look of intense pleasure swept over both their faces.

Did I look so enraptured when she fed on me?

More than likely.

I clenched my jaw, unease prickling in my stomach. This was insane. I'd never come across a human who'd needed more than one vampire to turn her. Was it because of the injuries she'd received? The strange patterns carved in her skin? Or was it something about the girl herself?

But it *was* working. Her wounds were healing again, the skin knitting slowly back together. Blood still seeped from them, but by the time Sol pulled away, the cuts had almost closed up. Not completely, like they should have, but she was no longer on the brink of death.

As the girl's breathing deepened and evened out, Sol and I both turned to Jerrett.

He cracked a smile despite the worry in his eyes. "Best for last, huh?"

"If it makes you feel better to think so. Yes. She needs more." Sol sat back.

Fortunately, Jerrett didn't hesitate or debate like I had. We all had our faults, but no one would ever accuse my oldest brother of overthinking things. The sleeve of his dark shirt was already rolled up to his elbow, and he pulled the girl into his lap as Sol stood.

Jerrett cradled the girl's body to him as she drank, murmuring softly in her ear. Finally, the multitude of cuts arrayed across her skin healed—though still not as perfectly as they should have.

Faint white scars remained, as if she'd received the wounds years ago.

When Jerrett moved to pull his wrist from her mouth, she mewled in protest, her tongue darting out to catch the last few drops as she lifted her head to chase the source.

"No more, sweetheart. Not tonight." He smoothed her hair back, his intense gaze locked on her face.

She blinked up at him slowly, her hazel irises glinting in the dim light. Red sparks flared within the flecks of brown and green as our vampire blood worked its way through her system.

Then her eyelids slid shut, and she fell limply back into Jerrett's arms. She was still covered in blood, but the color had returned to her cheeks. Her expression was peaceful.

I stood and rested a hand on Sol's shoulder.

Jerrett looked up at us. "What the hell just happened?"

My nostrils flared as I gritted my teeth. I had no answer for him. When we'd set out tonight to hunt a rogue shade, I couldn't have predicted how far off course the evening would go. If I had, would I still have come?

The girl would live, thanks to us.

But at what cost?

5

WILLOW

I DRAGGED my bleary eyes open.

Then my brow furrowed.

Where am I?

I wasn't in my bed in my tiny studio apartment. The view from the window wasn't the ugly, pigeon-filled alley I woke up to every morning. In fact, there was no view at all. There was no window—just a large door and several expensive-looking paintings hanging on walls painted a tasteful cream.

Swallowing hard, I moved to sit up, but a tug on my arms stopped me. Soft leather straps were wrapped around my wrists and secured to the headboard of the large four-poster bed.

"What the hell…?"

My shocked whisper was rough and gravelly. My breath came faster as I twisted as far as my binds would allow, craning my neck to take in my surroundings. This room was bigger than my entire apartment, and if I weren't scared out of my mind I probably would've admired the luxurious setting.

Where on earth am I?

My brain felt mushy, like cereal left to sit in milk for too long. I would've suspected a hangover, but I hardly ever drank at work —and besides, my body felt fine. No pounding headache accompanied my disorientation.

I struggled to sort through the previous night's events. Work had been busy, but not insane. An annoying creep had been hitting on a blonde girl, and I'd swooped in to rescue her. Then the guy had transferred his attention to me, following me around and staring down my shirt as if that might somehow charm me into going home with him. He'd been a pain in the ass, I could remember that well enough.

Right. I stayed late at the bar to make sure he was gone before I headed home.

Then…

My memory skipped. There was a blank, a black hole.

Pushing down my rising anxiety, I forced myself to work slowly through every minute I remembered.

I decided to walk home to save on cab fare. It was quiet, though a little cold. A nice enough night for a walk. Then there was a cold breeze, a noise behind me, and—

A rush of images suddenly flooded my brain, making my breath hitch.

The figure.

Shadowy and dark, yet somehow corporeal.

My fists striking its solid form. The crack of bone as it broke my ankle. Cold concrete beneath my body.

Nausea welled in my stomach as I recalled the pain and fear. Blood had gushed from my wounds as the dark shadow of a monster stooped over me, its claws tipped with red. I had felt the life slipping from my body.

I remembered the overwhelming sense of defeat. Like I'd

failed. Death had found me.

Or had it?

I felt plenty alive right now. The bite of the restraints digging into my skin reassured me I was still here.

Then a new memory struck me, sharper than the others.

A man's face.

The image flashed in my mind, and my body warmed. He'd been big and broad-shouldered. Handsome, with dark hair and bewitching, deep brown eyes. I could remember what his skin tasted like. Coppery. Salty.

How the hell do I know that?

We had been so close together. I remembered his face hovering over mine, the warmth of his breath wafting over my lips.

Then more pain.

Two other faces flashed through my mind.

One was a man with penetrating blue eyes, an eyebrow and lip piercing, and black hair that was shaved tight to his head on one side and long on top. He looked wild and untamed as a rock star, but his eyes were kind.

Had he helped me? Or had he tried to harm me?

My skin chilled. Monsters like that shadowy *thing* I'd seen weren't real. Maybe the massive brown eyed man or the man with blue eyes had been the one who really attacked me, and my brain had dealt with the assault by recasting him as something supernatural.

The third man had wavy blond hair and tanned skin. There had been something strange about his mesmerizing, light green eyes. What was it?

And who *were* those men? Why did I remember them so vividly? Where had I seen them before?

They weren't the type of people who frequented Osiris. The bar's clientele was mostly frat guys and businessmen trying to get lucky. Those three didn't fit into either of those categories.

My stomach dipped precipitously as a new thought rose to the surface of my fuzzy brain. Whether the shadow creature was real or a hallucination, those men's faces were the last thing I could remember before waking up in a strange room, strapped to a bed.

They were the reason I was here.

Panic shot through me, and I jerked my arms, fighting against my restraints.

I forced my body to stop struggling, forced myself to draw in long breaths through my nose. If I was going to get out of here alive, I needed to think rationally. Be strategic.

Slowly, I inched up the bed toward the headboard, giving the restraints on my wrists a little slack. My hands were bound too far apart for me to reach one with the other, so I couldn't do much to untie the straps. But maybe I could shimmy them loose.

Making a fist with my right hand, I rotated it slowly, giving a sustained pull against the strap binding me.

If I can just get a little more wiggle room, I can—

The thought died as a flash of intense, white-hot pain shot through me. My body bowed off the bed, and I thrashed against my bondage. My arms were wrenched behind me with a pop, and new pain flared. I'd nearly dislocated them.

An intense emptiness filled me, hunger I was sure would never be satisfied. I could consume the entire world, and the pain would never stop.

Sharp stabs of agony ripped through me, like someone had stuck a hot knife into my stomach and was driving it up and down. I didn't care about the men, didn't care about the creature made of shadow. All I could think about was ending this torture.

I need... something. I need it now.

Just when I thought I would pass out from the pain, the stabbing pangs of hunger faded, leaving me shaky and sweaty. I curled into a ball the best I could with my arms bound, as if making my stomach smaller would keep the gnawing hunger from returning.

I lay there for several long minutes, my breath returning to normal, my heart rate slowing.

A key turned in the lock of the large oak door.

My head whipped over in time to see the door handle rotating.

Shit! I was out of time. I didn't know what the men who'd taken me wanted from me, but it couldn't be anything good. *You don't attack and kidnap a stranger and then strap them to a bed because you want to be friends.*

As the door began to open, I let my head loll to one side, pressing my eyelids shut. Maybe if my captor thought I was asleep, I could take him by surprise when he got close enough. It probably wouldn't give me much of an upper hand, but it was the only hope I had right now.

Fear and despair tugged at me. Whoever had made these restraints was no beginner. They knew what they were doing.

They'd done this before.

I listened as my captor stepped into the room. The ache in my stomach was building again, that strange longing for something I didn't understand cutting through me so sharply I had to clench my jaw to keep from crying out.

Light footsteps approached me—lighter than they should've been to belong to any of the men I remembered. They'd all been so big, muscular, and solid. I tried to let my breathing deepen, to keep my arms from straining at the bonds.

The bed dipped, and a shock of awareness washed over me. I could *feel* the man's gaze on me like a physical weight. It tracked down my body, leaving goose bumps in its wake.

The mattress shifted again as he leaned toward me, and I moved.

My eyelids flew open as I turned my head sharply to face the intruder. It was the dark-haired man whose skin I could still taste. His striking brown eyes widened in surprise.

Moving on pure instinct, I lashed out. My arms were bound, but I still had my legs. I twisted and caught him off guard with a hard kick to his side. He grunted in pain, stumbling off the bed.

Holy shit. Maybe it was the adrenaline pumping through my body, but my kick had made more of an impact on this giant man than I'd expected.

Even so, it didn't stop him for long.

In the blink of an eye, he had me pinned to the bed under the weight of his muscular body. I struggled and writhed, trying to get a knee between his legs. But he was too damned heavy.

I reared up to bash my head into his face, but he pulled away quickly, dodging my blow. His thick legs straddled me, his hands pinning my shoulders down as he leaned forward with a snarl.

"Calm down, you wildcat!"

My breath hitched as his dark brown eyes blazed down at me.

That face. Those eyes.

I *had* seen this man before.

More than once.

6

WILLOW

"I KNOW YOU."

The whispered words escaped my lips unbidden, but their effect on the man was immediate. He drew back, looking almost guilty.

Confusion made my mind whirl. "How do I know you?"

I'd seen him before, somewhere other than in that one fuzzy memory. Where? When?

I saw him in a park once, didn't I? He was so strikingly handsome, I had to look again—but when I glanced back, he was gone.

Was that memory real? Or a part of my hallucinations?

"It's not important right now. You need to calm down. I'll explain everything soon." His voice was a deep rumble, the sound vibrating through his body and into mine.

This mountain of a man was big and strong, well over six feet tall and muscular. His face was broad and handsome, with a strong jawline. He had dark, shaggy hair that looked perfectly tousled, even though I was sure he never styled it, and he smelled like a mixture of leather and musk.

Holy shit. He doesn't look real. If he'd come up to me at Osiris, I would've given him my number in a heartbeat, something I'd never had the guts to do with any of the men who hit on me at work. Grace kept telling me it was time to start dating, but I was too scared to leap into that terrifying cesspool.

But the tall, dark man straddling me hadn't given me his number. He hadn't asked me on a date. He'd kidnapped me. It didn't matter how stupid-gorgeous he was if he wanted to kill me or rape me.

"I'll calm down when you untie me, you psycho!" I bucked my hips, barely moving his huge body.

If my fear was lending me extra strength, it wasn't enough. The weight of him on top of me was too much to fight against, but I threw everything I had into it, grunting and gasping as I tried to hit him with a knee, an elbow—anything.

With an annoyed sound, he leaned in closer, resting a thick forearm across my throat and effectively pinning my head to the mattress. I could still breathe, but panic flared inside me anyway.

"Are you done yet?" he growled, a spark of anger lighting in his eyes.

I nodded, the gesture tiny because of his weight on my throat. But the man either caught the small dip of my chin, or he recognized the look of defeat in my eyes. He sat back slowly, watching me warily, as if he expected me to resume my struggles any moment.

"There." His voice was softer now, the rumble like velvet over rocks. "That's better, isn't it?"

I gave another small nod, letting my body go soft beneath him. As the resistance drained from my muscles, I became unnervingly aware of everywhere we were connected. The weight of his pelvis rested on mine, and his thighs squeezed the sides of my body.

"I heard you scream." He narrowed his eyes, assessing me. "You're hungry, aren't you?"

My chin dipped for the third time. I didn't bother asking how he knew about the nameless, aching emptiness inside me.

Or maybe he's just asking if you want a sandwich, dummy.

My stomach rebelled at the thought. Along with my love of baking, I'd always had a deep love of eating—sweets especially, but I wasn't picky when it came to food. I loved it all.

But whatever sharp craving twisted inside my stomach, it wouldn't be satisfied by any kind of food I could think of.

The stranger must've noticed my throat convulsing as I fought down the bile rising into my mouth. His expression softened, regret and pity filling his eyes. He gripped my chin gently.

"I'm sorry, wildcat. I wouldn't have wished this life on you for the world. But I have something that will help."

Keeping his eyes trained on me, he reached for something on the bed behind him. He held it up, and I blinked.

"What—?" My voice cracked. I cleared my throat and tried again. "What is that?"

He didn't answer, but he really didn't need to. I'd seen enough hospital TV shows to know exactly what he had in his hands.

It was a bag, small and made of opaque white plastic. A brownish-red fluid sloshed around inside. But what I couldn't understand was the scent that came from it. Even through the plastic, I could pick up the rich, tangy flavor. It was the most tantalizing aroma I'd ever smelled—and I worked in a top-notch bakery.

This.

This was the thing I'd been craving, the thing my body had ached for, had tried to turn itself inside out for. I hadn't been able to give it a name until now.

I still couldn't name it aloud, but I bit my lip, my stomach contracting painfully as the thing I craved hovered so close, yet so far away. The man's gaze fell to my mouth, and for a moment, he stilled. Then his attention slid up to my eyes, and a rueful smile split his face as he waggled the bag.

"This will be... unsatisfying." He shook his head. "But it will keep the hunger at bay."

His words barely penetrated my brain, not that what he'd said made much sense anyway.

My gaze was locked on the small bag, as if nothing else in the world mattered anymore. My breath hitched when he brought it to his mouth, tearing a small hole in the plastic with his incisors.

Before I could speak, he wrapped a hand around the back of my neck, lifting me slightly as he pressed the bag to my lips. Thick, coppery liquid rushed into my mouth. My mind rebelled, refusing to think about what it was, but my body had no such reservations. I clamped my lips around the hole in the plastic and drank with long, hard pulls.

The liquid was cold, its rich flavor muted.

The man had been right. It *was* unsatisfying. Like eating junk food when I was craving a home-cooked meal. But right now it was all I needed. As the bag emptied, the burning in my stomach eased.

The man stood and picked up a second bag once I'd finished mine. I tracked its movements like a hungry wolf, biting my bottom lip before I looked up at him hopefully. I would've happily drained two dozen more of those bags. Although the bite of hunger was gone, the coppery scent elicited a craving I wasn't sure would ever be fully sated.

But this bag wasn't for me.

It was for him.

He tore through the plastic in the same way he'd done with mine and tipped the contents into his mouth. His dark eyes watched me as he drank, a challenge in his gaze. It was like he was daring me to… what? To look away in horror? To tell him what he was doing was wrong? How could I, when I'd just done the same thing?

And there was no way in hell I could look away.

I'd never seen anything so primally beautiful. I couldn't stop staring at the way his Adam's apple moved with each swallow, at the corded lines of his throat as he tipped his head back, the fullness of his lips. A slight growth of stubble adorned his sculpted cheeks and chin, making him look deliciously rough. One single, red drop escaped from the corner of his mouth, and his tongue darted out to catch it.

A small sound, almost a moan, reached my ears—and to my horror, I realized it had come from me.

The man's eyes darkened as his hand clenched tightly around the now-empty bag he held. I looked away quickly, a flush rising in my cheeks.

But the man didn't speak, and before I could utter a word, he plucked up the first empty bag from the bed and left.

The door closed, and the lock turned.

I was alone again.

Still alive.

And still tied to this damned bed.

7

SOL

I HAD NEVER BEGRUDGED Fate for taking my sight.

She'd given me so many things in return, it didn't feel right to mourn the loss of a single sense.

But as Malcolm carried the girl's unconscious body back to our house in Washington Heights, as her cherry and almond scent invaded my nostrils, I bit back a wave of jealousy that my brothers could see this stunning creature, and I could not.

I consoled myself with the knowledge that while they could smell her sweet blood and intoxicating skin, they missed the subtle notes of wine and honey that lingered in the background. That they couldn't sense the warm, bright shape of her aura like I could. That they weren't attuned to every small movement of her body.

Maybe it wasn't true, but in that moment, it was a lie I needed to believe. So I let myself believe it.

She was strong. That she'd attempted to fight a shade and held death at bay as long as she did was proof of that. Her strength would serve her well as she underwent the transition from human to vampire. I could remember my change vividly, the agony still as sharp in my memory as it'd been in reality. But as my brothers and I waited impatiently in the downstairs study, we heard only a few cries and moans from the guest room where we'd secured her.

The change was a deeply personal experience, and tradition dictated that none of us be present while she completed her transformation. But hearing her in distress set my teeth on edge, and I had to grip the arms of my chair to keep from flying up the stairs to comfort her.

When the sounds finally died down, Jerrett and I remained in the study as Malcolm tended to the girl, bringing her blood to help ease the pain.

Whether he admitted it or not, Malcolm was a natural leader. We had sworn our allegiance and our lives to him, and we followed his lead in all things—this included.

But by the time we'd made it back to the house, I had felt the tension radiating from his body. He'd had too much time to think as we shadow ran through the streets of New York in silence, and he already regretted what we'd done.

I knew why he felt that way, knew he viewed vampirism as a curse. But I'd never been able to see it like that. When I'd been bed-ridden as a human, dying of a mysterious disease, I had prayed for divine intervention.

I hadn't been finished with living yet—there was so much more still to do.

Some threads of life weren't meant to be cut short.

No matter what regrets Malcolm held, I was certain we'd made the right decision. To let something so precious wilt away like a neglected flower would've been a crime against Fate. The enchanting, mysterious woman had been put in our path for a reason, and we'd simply played out our destiny by saving her.

"What the fuck was that shade after? It carved those marks all over her body. Like it was a fucking preschooler trying to make confetti!"

Jerrett's chair scraped as he rose to pace back and forth across the room. His breath came short, and his heart thudded erratically.

I frowned and leaned back in my seat, remembering the shade's sickly aura. It'd felt like blackness and decay, and underneath that… something I wasn't quite able to identify. Something woody and light, at odds with everything else about the dark creature.

"I don't know, but something about that monster was very, very wrong. Once we deal with the girl, we need to return to the hunt. We'll find the shade and destroy it."

"Yeah?" Jerrett's footsteps stopped. "You know, I'm starting to think it's not the only one of those things in the city. It would explain why it's been so fucking hard to track. Because we're not picking up the trail of *one*, but *several*. That's why it's always one motherfucking step ahead of us."

He kicked a chair, and it skidded across the room, slamming into a wall and cracking.

I rubbed a hand down my face. Yuliya wouldn't be pleased to have to clean that mess up. She had an unlimited budget to replace broken pieces of furniture, but my temperamental brothers kept her busier than most housekeepers probably were—even though ours was aided by magic.

Malcolm's footsteps sounded on the stairs several minutes before he stormed into the room. Before he even spoke, I knew he was angry.

No, not just angry.

My brother was wound tight in a mass of self-loathing, frustrated desire, and rage. I should've expected it. He'd broken a vow tonight that meant more to him than almost anything.

She fed from each of us. We should all feel equally guilty.

But I couldn't bring myself to regret our actions one bit.

"Took you long enough!" Jerrett's aura churned with interest and agitation.

"How is she? Is her body handling the change all right?" I rose quickly, turning toward the door where Malcolm stood.

"Well enough to land a kick on me before I could give her a blood bag." He chuckled, his aura lightening briefly.

Jerrett let out a low whistle. "Damn. She's fierce. Did you see the scrapes on her knuckles too? She tried to fight the shade. I'm sure of it."

He was right. My heart swelled with pride for the girl, although I barely knew her. But the moment of levity was broken as Malcolm stalked farther into the room, his dark mood returning.

"We shouldn't have done this," he ground out, his footsteps heavy. He smelled of stale blood from the blood bag, and of the girl.

What is it about her scent? Something about it draws me in, makes me hunger for her in a way I've never felt before.

"We should have stuck to the plan and gone after the shade." Malcolm leaned on the mantel over the fireplace as the fire popped and cracked within. "*How* could I have let her drink from me? I swore I'd never turn another human, and I should've kept my promise. It was a mistake. A stupid mistake."

"What were we supposed to do? Let her die?" Jerrett shot back, his voice dropping into an angry growl.

Each man's body temperature rose slightly, and I tensed.

My brothers rarely fought, but when they did, it could get out of hand quickly. I hoped it wouldn't come to that. If Yuliya was upset about the chair, she'd be absolutely furious about having to scrub bloodstains out of the carpet.

"I don't know." Malcolm's voice was thick. Then he cursed under his breath. "No! Of course not."

Jerrett huffed. "Exactly. And since we did turn her, she's our responsibility."

"A responsibility we don't need. One I don't want. We're hunters, and we have a job to do. We need to get back to tracking that shade before it attacks again."

"So what do we do?" I asked.

Malcolm was silent for a moment. A vampire's heart usually beat much slower than a human's, but his sped up now, thrumming powerfully in his chest.

"We make sure she finishes the transition safely. Keep her strapped down, because the wildcat fights back—then we let her go." He sank into his usual chair near the fire.

I could hear Jerrett's teeth grinding behind me, feel the fresh wave of anger radiating from him.

"Cut her loose? Like she's a stray fucking cat we don't want? No way in hell. She's one of us now. We did this to her. She needs our help!"

"We saved her life. That's enough," Malcolm muttered.

"*Enough*? Are you fucking kidding me?"

"Of course, I'm not kidding."

"Well, then I guess you're just insane. I'm not letting her go."

Malcolm blew out a heavy breath. "I know you may not believe this, brother, but I'm not just thinking of myself. It's better for her this way too. We have our lives. She has hers. Just because we turned her doesn't mean we have to drag her along on the hunt with us. She doesn't deserve that."

"You're both forgetting something."

I spoke quietly, but Malcolm and Jerrett stopped bickering and turned to me. They'd known me long enough to understand I wasn't one for wasted words—when I did speak, it was because I had something important to say.

"Yeah, what's that?" Jerrett asked.

"We're supposed to declare her."

A moment of stunned silence met my words. I could feel Malcolm's regret looming like a fourth person in the room as he scrubbed a hand through his hair.

"No. I won't do that." His voice was hard.

I nodded, resting my forearms on the back of my chair. "Understandable. I was just pointing out that we're *supposed* to declare her."

"Shit," Jerrett muttered.

"That decides it," Malcolm said grimly. "If she stays with us, she's more likely to be discovered by the court. And I will *not* put her through that. On her own, she can stay under the radar forever. I know there are undeclared vampires living in secret. If she's smart, no one will ever find her."

"Shit. Fucking fuck!"

"Yes, that about sums it up." Malcolm's voice was tinged with sadness. "Look, I'm not suggesting we throw her out on the streets without giving her any help. We can keep her supplied with blood bags. She'll never have to worry about that."

Jerrett hissed through his teeth, lashing out to punch a hole in a wall for the second time tonight. At least it was our own property he was destroying this time, although I wasn't sure Yuliya would see it that way.

"Fine! We'll let her go. But just for the record, I fucking hate this."

Malcolm grunted in response, a sound of commiseration and assent. A heavy silence fell over the room as the fire continued to snap and pop.

My thoughts drifted upstairs to the girl.

Her unique cherry and almond scent lingered in my nostrils even now. I wondered how she was doing after her first feeding. How she was handling the transition. It wasn't an easy process, especially on top of the trauma of a near-death experience. I knew that from experience.

She's strong.

That thought kept rising to the top of my mind as the warmth of the fire bathed my face.

She's strong.

She must be, to have survived as long as she did tonight. To have fought that shade even when she had no chance against it. Hell, she was strong to have fought Malcolm. His size and commanding presence intimidated even powerful vampires.

I admired her strength. Her spunk.

And something told me even if we tried to let her go, it wouldn't be that easy.

8

WILLOW

As soon as my captor left the room, I resumed struggling. The coppery taste of the liquid lingered on my tongue, taunting me, but my brain shut down any attempt I made to analyze what it was. Every time I did, my stomach threatened to reject what I'd so happily consumed as waves of nausea and horror rolled through me.

What the hell is happening to me?

I pulled so hard at the straps, I feared I really would dislocate my arms. But it was no good. The bonds were unbreakable. No matter how much I thrashed or struggled, they wouldn't budge. Whoever my captor was, he'd planned well for this.

Maybe I'm not the first person he's done this to. Jesus. What happened to the others?

I let my head flop back to the bed, closing my eyes. My wrists were raw and bruised from my struggles, but I had nothing to show for it. Maybe a better option would be to play nice, to give this man whatever he wanted and hope that he'd eventually let me go.

Flashes of hot and cold washed over my skin, bathing my body in sweat and goose bumps. The hunger pangs had faded, but now it felt like there were insects crawling through my body—a strange prickling sensation that spread out through my limbs. As I wriggled uncomfortably on the plush mattress, I wished for the first time in months that I were back in Ohio.

I'd been so happy to leave, so proud of myself for picking up and starting my life over in the city I'd always dreamed about. But maybe I never should've come.

My apartment in Brooklyn was a tiny shithole, I was exhausted and stretched thin all the time from working two jobs, and I ate ramen at least four nights a week. But none of that had bothered me, because I was pursuing my dreams. The past eight months in New York, I'd felt more alive than I had for the nine years I'd been married to Kyle.

We'd married the summer after I graduated high school, and I had been so *sure* I loved him, so certain he was everything I needed in a man. But what the hell did I know? I was a kid.

And he wasn't a man. He was a boy.

My parents had thrown a fit, but I hadn't listened to them. I'd never been close to my father, even less so to my stepmom, so their disapproval had only bolstered my confidence that I was making the right choice marrying Kyle. They'd refused to come to our small wedding and had cut me out of their lives afterward.

Years later, as the depth and breadth of the mistake I'd made slowly began to sink in, I often picked up the phone and punched in my dad's cell number, only to hang up before he answered. Too much time had passed, and too many harsh words had been exchanged between us, for me to turn to my parents for help and support.

So I'd gathered my courage on my own and finally told Kyle I couldn't stay with him anymore. That I needed more than the half-life we were living together.

His lack of resistance to my request for a divorce was more heartbreaking than if he'd fought me on it. I still didn't know if his apathetic response was because he truly didn't care about me anymore, or because he was certain I'd fail in my attempt at a better life and come crawling back to him.

Sadness sat like a brick on my chest as I stared up at the ceiling in this unfamiliar room. My blood continued to prickle, as if all my limbs had fallen asleep. Heaviness weighed down my eyelids.

I'd wanted to prove Kyle wrong. To show him, and myself too, that I could make it in New York City. That I could achieve the daunting goals I set for myself.

I wished I had more to show for my attempts than being tied up on a stranger's bed.

Thank God, Kyle can't see me now.

Still shivering, I drifted into a restless sleep. Images of the shadow monster and the three beautiful men played in my mind over and over, taunting me.

Daring me to guess which were the angels and which were the devils.

When my eyes opened again, the itchy feeling in my muscles was gone.

The room looked the same as it had when I dozed off, and I realized I had no idea what time it was—or even what day it was. Had it been several hours since my attack on that dark street, or a few days? Was I even in New York anymore?

I'd become so accustomed to the constant ambient light and sound that seemed to exist almost everywhere in the city that it was strange not to sense them. This place was too dark, too quiet.

The key jiggled in the lock again, and I jumped. He was back.

I took a deep breath. *Play nice, Willow. Stay calm and maybe you'll get out of this in one piece.*

The tall, broad-shouldered man stepped into the room, but this time he wasn't alone. The other two men from my dream stepped in behind him. The first one had a shock of black hair, shaved on one side and longer on top, flopping down over his stunningly blue eyes. His lip and eyebrow were pierced, his features sharp as cut glass. He looked like a rock star, and the tattoos creeping up his neck only added to the effect.

The second one with the strange green eyes didn't make eye contact, but I somehow felt like he was peering straight into my soul. His golden-brown hair was wavy, and he had a perfectly shaped mouth and a small dimple in his chin.

My jaw fell slack, all the threats and bargains I'd prepared dying on my tongue. These men were beautiful, otherworldly—and terrifying.

Before I could force words from my parched lips, the rock star stepped up to the side of the bed. He cast a reproachful glance over his shoulder at the tall, dark-haired one who'd visited me before, then leaned over to unwind the restraints on my wrists.

"Careful. She kicks." The first man's gravelly voice was dry.

"Yeah? Funny, she's not kicking me. Maybe it's just something about your charming personality that makes people want to kick your ass," the rock star shot back.

A grumbling sound was the only response, but I hardly heard it. The rock star's face was only inches from mine as he removed the restraints, giving my aching wrists some relief. His blue eyes danced with humor at my stunned expression, one corner of his mouth lifting as he stared down at me.

My breath hitched. The bright blue of his irises were so close to mine, and the smoke and clove scent of him seemed to envelop me. I blinked, trying to stop the sensation of falling into him as though gravity had somehow been reversed. I kept my eyes squeezed shut until I felt him pull away, his low chuckle lingering in my ear.

As I sat up slowly, the first man stepped forward and offered me another bag. Even though the smell made my mouth water, I shook my head. I couldn't deny what it was any longer, and now that the pain in my body and the cramping in my stomach had eased, the rational part of my mind was taking over again.

And it wanted nothing to do with any of this.

"Suit yourself, wildcat." He shook the bag gently. "But you'll need to feed again before too long. Your body has been through a lot, it needs nourishment. And I've seen what you're like when you're hangry."

My gaze whipped up to his face, startled.

Did he just... make a joke?

For a heartbeat, a ghost of a smile whispered across his face, then his dark brows pulled together again, his dour expression returning.

"No, thanks. I'll—I'll be fine. What happened? Why did you bring me here?" I licked my lips. "What do you want with me?"

"Nothing. Apparently." Rock star glared at the tall, dark one, who ran a hand through his hair in irritation.

The green-eyed man tilted his head, gazing down at me. Or *through* me? His irises were pure white instead of black, and I wondered if he was blind. But if that were true, why did he seem to perceive so much?

"You were attacked," he said gently.

I clenched my hands, fear sliding through me like poison. "By you?"

"No. By a shade. A dangerous supernatural creature, undead and powerful. We found you and saved you."

The biggest man grunted, turning away from the bed. The muscles of his back bunched with tension.

Dangerous supernatural? Undead?

I forced my brain to try to process those words instead of dissolving into a gibbering mess.

"You… saved me?" I repeated dumbly.

I strained to remember anything helpful, but all I could access were flashes of the shadow monster and the three men's faces.

Then something new sparked in my memory. A taste. Like the liquid in the bag, but hotter, more satisfying. I had drunk it and felt high for the first time in my life. I'd never done drugs, not even in high school, but I was sure the feeling I'd experienced had been better than any drug could produce. It'd been intoxicating. Addictive.

"Yeah, we did," said the rock star. He brushed the dark lock of hair out of his eyes, but it fell back into the exact same spot. "You were in bad shape, sweetheart."

"How did you kill that thing?" I asked.

Goose bumps ran up my arms as I recalled the hulking, shadowy creature. It had been ephemeral and yet solid, and so dark that no amount of light could illuminate it clearly.

The first man sighed, turning back to face us. "We didn't kill it. That was our aim, but it escaped. We had to let it go to save your life. You were bleeding out on the pavement." The line between his brows deepened. "You had minutes left."

"How did you save me?" I asked.

A memory of claws raking down the front of my body assaulted me, and my breath hitched. I looked down at myself, searching for bandages or wounds. I was stiff and sore, but I could find no obvious signs of any attack. Except…

I narrowed my eyes, staring at my arms.

A network of fine white scars crisscrossed my skin, so faint I hadn't noticed them earlier. They seemed to form some kind of pattern, but I had no idea what it was. Had each of these scars been a wound from the creature? How had they healed already?

The blond man sighed, sitting on the edge of the bed and resting a hand on my ankle. I could've lashed my foot out and kicked him in the face, but I was feeling less and less like attacking these men. Whatever the hell was going on here, they were the only lifeline I had at the moment.

"You were too far gone for medical intervention. You'd lost so much blood. We had to turn you." His smooth voice was almost apologetic.

The words took a moment to sink in, and when they finally did, they drilled into my brain like a hot poker.

Oh God.

This wasn't a joke.

It wasn't a misunderstanding.

It wasn't a bad dream.

That opaque plastic bag I'd sucked so greedily from had been full of blood. I had drained the entire thing and liked it. I'd *needed* it.

I stared up into the man's kind, sightless eyes, my heart

stuttering in my chest. Helpless tears burned in my throat as every truth I thought I'd known about the world crumbled around me.

"Turn me?" I whispered. "You mean I'm a… a…"

My throat closed. The word wouldn't come.

9

JERRETT

"A VAMPIRE," Mal bit out curtly, his nostrils flaring.

I rolled my eyes. *For fuck's sake.*

His anger was directed inward. He hated that he'd agreed to turn the girl. He was only being a dick because he felt like shit about what we'd done, but still.

Give the girl a damn minute to process it, huh?

The woman's face drained of color, her hazel eyes widening. Shock reflected in their depths, but resignation was there too. She'd known, even before Mal opened his big mouth. She wasn't stupid. She was just scared.

A flush worked its way across her skin, tingeing her chest and cheeks a soft, dusky pink. Goddamn, she was fucking beautiful. She was stunning, even in the midst of her shock. Even as she realized she was one of us.

The corner of my lip rose in a half-snarl.

No. Not *one of us.*

Mal had made that plenty fucking clear. We weren't keeping her, as much as I wished we could. Sol and Mal had both made good points about why this was the better course of action, but I still thought they were wrong. Mal was a great hunter—cool and calm in a fight, smart and careful. But when it came to things like this, he was a fucking mess. He tried to use his head to make decisions that should be left up to the heart and gut.

"Vampire..."

The girl repeated the word as if her lips had never formed those sounds before. She blinked then said it again, as a question this time.

"Vampire?"

"Yes. Like I just told you," Mal said impatiently. He rocked on his feet, like he couldn't wait to get out of here.

Her eyes narrowed, the flush on her cheeks deepening. "Well, *excuse me*. I need a minute to deal with that insane news, okay?"

I smiled, tugging my lip ring into my mouth. Fuck, I liked this girl. Anybody who talked back to Mal when he deserved it was all right in my book.

Sol squeezed her ankle. "Take whatever time you need. We know it's a lot to handle. But please remember, we did it to save you. You're alive now because we turned you. I hope knowing that can help you come to terms with this."

"Hey, it's not so bad," I put in, trying to reassure her. "I've been a vamp for a long time, and I do okay."

"*Not so bad?*" She gave a breathy, humorless laugh. "This would never have happened in Ohio," she muttered.

I quirked a smile. "Eh, I dunno about that. There's a pretty big clan right outside Cincinnati. And yeah, it's not so bad. You'll crave blood sometimes, but you don't need to drink it every day to stay alive. You can still subsist mostly on human food. And when you do need blood, you won't have to kill to get it." I gestured to Mal and Sol. "We don't. All three of us took a vow not to drink from unwilling humans. We steal blood bags from hospitals when we need to."

"From hospitals?"

I bit back a grin. It was obvious this girl was smart and capable. But it was like the revelation of her new supernatural status had sapped her brainpower. All she could do was repeat what we said in a slightly higher register.

Mal studied the woman, his dark eyes thoughtful.

"What do you do for a living?" he asked.

Her gaze flew to him, and for a second, it looked like she was struggling to remember the answer. The idea that she'd had a life and a job before all this seemed to catch her by surprise.

"I work at a bar. Osiris," she said slowly. "That's what I was doing before I got attacked. I always work late, so I'm used to walking home in the dark."

Mal dipped his head. "That's good. So you're used to evening hours. You can keep working, as long as you don't go out during the day."

The girl's eyes narrowed in anger. I didn't blame her. My brother was a good man, but his bedside manner could use a lot of fucking work.

"That's all you have to say?" she hissed. "You turned me into a…" She swallowed hard but forged ahead, her anger overriding her fear. "A *vampire*. And now the best you can do is tell me it'll all be okay because I can still work as a cocktail waitress?"

I tried to cut through the tension, even though Mal kind of deserved the wrath she was throwing his way.

"I know it sucks, but my brother's right, sweetheart. The best thing you can do is go back to your old life. Just do what you were doing before you were turned and stay under the radar.

Don't let *anyone* know you're a vampire. It's the safest thing for you. Trust me."

The girl turned to face me, a look of abject despair on her face. A knife twisted in my heart, and I could've thrown Mal off the fucking roof for making us do this.

"I... I work at a bakery too. Will I not be able to do that anymore?"

I grimaced. "Honestly, probably not. But you'll be able to keep working at the bar. You work nights there, right? So it won't be a problem. Just act like nothing happened."

"Act like nothing happened," she whispered, a tear slipping down her cheek. She was back to repeating what we said again, but this time it wasn't even remotely funny. It was heartbreaking.

I wanted to wrap her in my arms and hold her. To tell her that everything would be all right. My brothers seemed to be struggling with similar feelings, if the thickening of the air was any indication. But none of us moved.

"You'll be all right, sweetheart," I said softly. "You're a survivor. We all saw that firsthand. It'll be hard at first, but you'll adjust to your new life. Hell, maybe you'll even enjoy it one day. There *are* a few perks."

From the corner of my eye, I caught Sol nodding slightly. The three of us had each struggled with various aspects of our vampirism, Mal most of all, but we'd come out the other side stronger than ever.

She would too.

Fuck. I didn't even know this girl's name, but I cared for her already. Though Mal was acting like an ass-wipe, I knew he did too. So did my youngest brother.

It made sense. The bond between a vampire and someone he or she turned could be a powerful thing. It wasn't always strong, but the transformation forged a connection that would never fade.

You couldn't give someone a part of yourself, something that changed the very essence of who they were, and both walk away untouched. That wasn't how it worked. This woman with the soft hazel eyes and shining chocolate-brown hair was connected to all three of us now. And that bond would likely grow stronger if we spent more time together.

Which, of course, was why my brother was in such a goddamned hurry to kick her out. He knew if we didn't do it soon, everything would get messier and more difficult.

"Do you have a boyfriend? Husband? Children?" Mal asked. His voice was clinical, but his eyes burned with interest.

She stared at him for a second before answering slowly. "No. I… did. I'm divorced. But we hadn't had kids yet."

My eyebrows shot up in surprise. She was divorced? She looked young, which meant she must've gotten married *very* young. And what fucking idiot let this stunning woman go?

"That's good too. You won't have to try to explain the change in your behavior to a loved one. It will make things easier for you."

The woman's face paled, sadness washing over her features. I resisted the urge to punch Mal in the face. I knew he was trying to help, but every word out of his damn mouth only made things worse.

Before I could say anything, Mal dropped the blood bag he'd brought on the nightstand. The girl stared at it as it landed with a dull thud.

"You'll need to feed again before you go. We'll call you a car as soon as the sun sets, and the driver will take you home. Give him your address, and we'll make sure you stay supplied with regular deliveries of blood."

Mal paused, a war raging across his features. Probably trying to think of something to say that would ease his conscience. But in the end he settled for turning sharply on his heel and stalking out without another word.

Sol went to follow but hesitated in the doorway, turning back to the woman.

"I'm Sol, by the way." His mouth tilted into a sad smile. "I'm sorry we had to meet under these circumstances, but I have to admit, I'm not sorry we met. What is your name, sweet one?"

"Willow," she said, her gaze trapped by his green eyes. "Willow Pear—er, Tate."

"Willow." My brother repeated the name, letting it roll off his tongue like he was tasting it. "It was very nice to meet you. Remember, keep what you are a secret. Please be safe."

She didn't respond, and a moment later, he slipped out the door after Mal.

Willow. It was a beautiful name. It suited her perfectly.

She bends. She doesn't break.

I looked back down at her pale, serious face, suddenly feeling a little nervous—an emotion I hadn't felt around a woman in a long-ass fucking time.

Clearing my throat, I brushed the hair out of my eyes. "Yeah. Uh, I better go too."

Willow nodded, but still didn't speak. She just stared up at me with her huge hazel eyes, an avalanche of emotions cascading through them.

Ah, fuck it. Mal got his way on everything. What he doesn't know won't hurt him.

With my gaze still locked on hers, I sat on the edge of the bed and ran a knuckle down the side of her face. Her skin was soft, warm, and smooth. Letting my eyes drift closed, I leaned forward to inhale her sweet scent one more time.

Cherry and almond. Fucking perfect.

I turned my head and pressed a chaste kiss to her cheek. To my surprise, she let out a hitched breath, shivering at my touch. The responding rush in my body was immediate, and I pulled back quickly, fisting my hands. Fuck, I wanted to bury my fingers in her hair and taste every inch of her skin.

"Sorry, sweetheart." I forced myself to stand and back away. "It wasn't meant to be."

I left the room, aching for something more than just blood. I wanted *her*. Her soft skin, her fierce spirit, the mystery behind her eyes.

I wanted all of it.

But instead, I had to let her go.

Goddamnit, Mal. You're gonna owe me for this forever.

10

WILLOW

The tall man, the one who'd never introduced himself, returned to the bedroom after a while. He unlocked the door—which didn't have a locking mechanism on the inside, I'd discovered—and gestured for me to follow him without a word.

My legs were wobbly, and I stumbled slightly as we walked down a long hallway. He helped me regain my balance and then guided me downstairs with a hand at my elbow. I honestly wasn't sure if his grip on my arm was meant as a gesture of chivalry or control.

Maybe a bit of both.

The house was large and luxurious, with high ceilings and tasteful decor. When we reached the front door, he handed me a small insulated pack full of blood bags and finally broke his silence to give me instructions on how to store them properly.

Then he ushered me into the waiting car outside and stood on the dark street watching us drive away. I tried to resist, but I couldn't stop myself from craning my neck to keep my gaze on him until we turned a corner, and he dropped out of sight.

I'll probably never see him again. Never see any of them.

That thought should've comforted me.

And it did... sort of.

The rest of the ride home was a blur. I made conversation with the driver on autopilot, though he seemed as unenthusiastic about it as I was. But silence was worse, so I kept up a stream of inane chatter as we drove down brightly lit streets to my neighborhood in Brooklyn. He refused payment or a tip when he dropped me off, insisting his employers wouldn't like it—they'd already taken care of everything.

Then he pulled away, and I stared up at my run-down apartment building. It looked just the same as it had last time I'd seen it. So did the rest of the street.

As though everything was perfectly normal.

Except nothing would ever be *normal* for me again. Not since Sol, Jerrett, and the intensely moody man they called "brother" came into my life. All three of them were so ungodly beautiful, yet so unnerving at the same time. Were all vampires like them, or were they special even amongst their own kind? It didn't seem possible for all vampires to be so striking. If they were, wouldn't humans have picked up on their presence a long time ago?

I huffed a laugh.

I'll take "Things I Never Thought I'd Say" for two hundred, please, Alex.

What I really wanted, more than anything in the world, was to go upstairs, fall asleep, and wake up tomorrow with no bags full of blood in my refrigerator. No network of scars winding across my body. I wanted to marvel at the strange dream I'd had, dash out the door because I was late for work, and spend the morning baking sweet confections in Carly's shop.

But as hard as I wished, I was sure that wouldn't happen.

I walked slowly up the two flights to my unit's floor. It was almost disorienting to step back into my crappy studio apartment. I felt a little like I'd broken into a stranger's home, as though I no longer truly belonged here. Rubbing my eyes, I stumbled inside, a bone-deep exhaustion tugging at me.

I passed by the full-length mirror on the wall by the door, and my steps slowed. Then I backed up, my eyes widening as I came to stand in front of it.

Is that... me?

It *was* me, of course, though I was a bit ragged around the edges and appeared slightly crazed. But I also looked different somehow, as if someone had taken a picture of me then applied a bunch of crazy filters to it. Flecks of gold and red glittered in my hazel irises, making my eyes seem to dance with light. My dark hair was fuller, shinier, and my skin was so smooth it looked like porcelain. I stuck out my tongue, just to be sure the reflection in the mirror was actually real.

She stuck out her tongue right back at me, and I rolled my eyes, continuing my perusal of myself in the mirror.

As my gaze drifted downward, something else stuck me. I wasn't wearing the purple top and dark skinny jeans I'd left the bar in. The clothes I wore now were a similar style, which was why I hadn't noticed earlier, but they most definitely weren't mine.

My breath hitched as the full implications of that dawned on me. Of *course,* I wasn't wearing the clothes I'd had on when I was attacked. Based on the vampires' description, and my own awful memories of the event, that outfit would've been shredded and soaked in blood.

Which meant one or more of the brothers had undressed me and put me in these new clothes.

The thought of their hands on my body should've turned my stomach, but a surprising and entirely unwelcome flush worked its way up my chest instead.

God, Willow. Get ahold of yourself.

My blush deepened as embarrassment flooded me. Maybe stress or the recent extreme change in my body was sending my hormones out of whack. I was normally too sensible to let myself develop an attraction to beautiful, dangerous men.

But the truth was, the rush of warmth when I thought of them wasn't just because of their stunning good looks. In the short time I'd spent with them, each of them, even Mr. Tall, Dark, and Cranky, had gazed at me with tenderness and fierce protectiveness.

No one had looked at me that way in a long time. Probably not since before I married Kyle.

I hadn't realized how much I missed it. That feeling of being wanted. Protected.

Screwing my eyes shut, I rested my forehead against the mirror.

Seriously, Willow. Cut it out. Or did you forget the part where they kicked you out and abandoned you to deal with this insane new world on your own?

That was the metaphorical bucket of ice water I needed. Any warm feelings I'd been feeling toward the three brothers died under a crushing wave of reality. Gritting my teeth, I moved away from the mirror, stopping in the kitchen to deposit my new… snacks… in the fridge.

Those three men claimed they'd saved my life. But all they'd done was ruin it.

I changed out of the clothes that weren't mine into a pair of comfy sweats and an old t-shirt. Then I settled onto the bed, staring out the small window at the alley below. At a world I no longer understood.

When the horizon began to glow pink, my eyelids drooped. Though I was exhausted, I had enough sense to fasten a heavy blanket to the window to stop the light from coming in with the dawn. Then I curled up under my blanket, pulling it over my head.

For once, I was glad I couldn't afford a place with giant windows and a great view.

I WOKE IN THE EVENING, just as the sun was beginning to set.

A slight haze of warm orange light slipped through a small crack between the blanket and the wall. I lay on my back watching the light turn from orange to gray to black.

Finally, I slipped out of bed, padding over to the closet for a change of clothes.

A sudden pang of guilt stabbed me.

My bakery job. I hadn't shown up to Carly's Confections in at least two days.

I checked my cell to find that Carly, the owner, had left me several concerned messages. She didn't sound mad, which only made the guilt worse. It wasn't like me to miss work, and she knew that. She was probably worried out of her mind, assuming the worst.

Or at least, the worst thing she can conceive of.

The word "vampire" had probably never entered her thoughts.

I tapped the button on the screen to call her back and chewed on my lip while it rang.

"Willow!" Her squeaky voice sounded a little breathless. "Willow, honey, are you all right?"

"Yeah. Yeah, I am."

She peppered me with a barrage of questions, talking even faster than she normally did. This five-foot-nothing woman had more energy than anyone I'd ever met. When she finally slowed down, I reassured her I was fine, but told her I'd come down with a bad stomach bug that had knocked me out of commission for a few days. I apologized over and over again, but Carly wouldn't hear it.

"You can't help it if you're sick! Take as much time as you need. Your body will thank you for it," she said, before making me promise to call her if I got any worse.

As I pressed the "end call" button, her words struck me. How much time *would* I need? A week? A year? I likely couldn't ever go back to work at the bakery; Jerrett had told me that. If I'd been smarter, I would've made up some reason to quit right now.

In a few days, my excuse of illness would wear out, and I'd have to come up with a better explanation for why I wasn't ever coming back. But I couldn't bring myself to do that yet. I needed to hold onto the illusion that my old life wasn't totally over for just a little while longer.

I glanced at my tiny kitchen, a narrow galley set off from the main room, and my stomach rumbled. I supposed it was technically breakfast time according to my bizarre new schedule, but I didn't really care.

There's never a bad time for cupcakes.

Baking was my go-to activity when I was stressed. It soothed me. There was something incredibly comforting about the mindlessness of mixing and stirring, measuring and pouring.

My fridge was pretty bare—not counting the blood bags—but

I always kept basic baking ingredients in the pantry. Thirty minutes later, twelve perfectly risen cupcakes cooled on a rack while I whipped up some butter and powdered sugar.

I added four drops of red food coloring to the frosting, then hesitated. The intensely saturated droplets dripped down the fluffy white peaks like bloodstains. Hunger stirred in my belly, followed by an answering wave of nausea as my mind grappled with my new reality. I groped blindly on the counter for another bottle of food coloring, adding blue on top of the red. I stirred it quickly, turning the frosting a vibrant purple.

Better.

Taking my time, I piped out intricate designs on the cupcakes, letting the activity calm me. Finally, I picked one up, tapped it against another in a kind of toast, and took a bite.

My eyes nearly rolled back in my head.

It was delicious. Unbelievably good.

Cupcakes had been one of the first recipes I'd mastered when I started baking. I'd gotten pretty damn good at them, but these tasted better than anything I'd baked before. The soft and springy vanilla sponge was like heaven on my tongue, the frosting intensely sweet without being saccharine.

Wow. What on earth did I do differently with this recipe?

As I licked my fingers, polishing off the last sweet vestiges of purple frosting, it struck me. I hadn't done anything different. The recipe was the same. The cupcakes were the same. It was *me* who had changed.

Jerrett had said there were some perks to being a vampire. Maybe a heightened sense of taste and smell was one of them.

A small breath of relief fell from my lips as I packed the remaining cupcakes away. This was the first aspect of being a vampire that actually seemed pleasant. And at least I wouldn't have to live off blood alone.

Thank God. A life without cake wouldn't be worth living.

What other perks and drawbacks were there to this strange new life? What did being a vampire really mean?

Giving in to my gnawing curiosity, I pulled out my beat-up laptop and flopped back onto my bed. There must be some information out there that could help me.

Is there some kind of vampire survival guide or something?

I tried a few Google searches and found a lot of information on vampires. Some of it seemed true, like the sensitivity to the sun. That had been verified by the brothers. Some was totally fictional—like vampires having no heartbeat and not being able to digest anything but blood. I could see for myself those myths were incorrect.

Very little of what I found was helpful.

I pressed the laptop closed, the full weight of my situation finally bearing down on me like a pile of rubble. Trapping me. Suffocating me.

Feeling more alone than I ever had in my life, I set the laptop on the nightstand and crawled under the covers, curling up into a tight ball. I pulled the blanket up over my head, tears stinging my eyes and streaming down my cheeks.

What is my life now? How am I supposed to do this?

And why had the most beautiful men I'd ever met cursed me to live like this?

11

WILLOW

Over the next week, I tried hard to follow the vampire brothers' instructions and get on with my life.

It pained me to admit it, but the dark-haired one was right. Since leaving Kyle and moving to a new city on my own, I had so few attachments left that no one noticed the change in me. No one called or knocked on my door, wondering what had happened to me.

The job at Osiris had always been my survival job, while the bakery had been my passion. But since I couldn't leave home during the day anymore, the bar was my only chance to maintain a semblance of my old life. I was determined to go back to work right away and act as if nothing had happened to me.

If I acted like I was okay, maybe I'd start to *feel* okay.

But all the determination in the world couldn't comfort me as my next shift at the bar approached. The knot in my stomach kept tightening. I hadn't been around people since my transformation, and the bar was always packed to the brim, even on weeknights.

What would I do if a craving came over me, and I couldn't control myself? The blood bags were fine, but there was something lacking in them. The thought of drinking fresh blood made my heart hammer with equal parts excitement and horror.

At Osiris, I'd be in a room full of them. A room full of potential victims. A room full of witnesses. It was a disaster waiting to happen.

So I took the coward's route and called out for a few nights. I used the same excuse I'd given Carly, and although the bar manager, Tony, was nowhere near as sweet about it as she'd been, he didn't give me too much flack.

I spent the next several days locked up in my apartment sleeping, binge-watching trashy shows on Netflix, stress-baking, and staring out the window.

By the time the seventh evening rolled around, I was going completely stir crazy. I didn't know what my new life as a vampire meant, but I was positive I didn't want this to be it. Anything was better than staying locked up in my apartment like some kind of pariah.

My self-imposed exile was wearing on my sanity, and it'd only been a few days. I'd never last a year, let alone hundreds of years, living like this. Being around people might be difficult, but I was growing more certain I could handle it.

I wasn't scheduled to work until the next evening, but I craved the comfort of someplace familiar. So at around 11 p.m., I threw on one of the only dresses I owned—a stretchy black number with thin shoulder straps that hugged my curves and fell to about mid-thigh. I'd bought it when I first moved to New York but had only worn it once. I didn't go out much, so I'd had few opportunities.

My worry about snapping and attacking someone had waned, but just to be on the safe side, I pulled a blood bag from the fridge, poked a hole in it, and drained it swiftly. I tried not to enjoy the coppery taste as it slid down my throat—tried to ignore the way my incisors grew longer as I drank, as if called by some primal part of me.

After pulling my dark hair back into a ponytail and slipping on a pair of heels, I headed for the bar. The cool night air was a welcome change from the stuffiness of my apartment.

For the first few minutes, I darted my gaze around furtively, convinced I must have a neon sign above me flashing "Different! Does not belong!"

But no one crossed the street to avoid me or shrank away in fear at the sight of me. A few men eyed me up and down as I passed, but that was it.

Osiris was packed as usual. I made my way through the crowd and sidled up to the bar. Pete, one of my favorite bartenders, glanced up at me then did a double-take. He was probably surprised to see me in a dress. My usual work outfit was a simple top and nice jeans, the most basic ensemble Tony would let me get away with.

"Damn, you look good, Willow!" he called, leaning over the bar toward me. "Hey, you feeling better?"

"Much. Thanks." I grinned, almost giddy at the first human interaction I'd had in days.

I ordered the fanciest cocktail on the menu. I'd only had it once before, when I'd first started working at Osiris and was in training. But I wanted to see what it would taste like with my newly enhanced senses.

Speaking of which...

I wrinkled my nose. There apparently was a downside to every upside about this whole vampire business. My enhanced sense of smell and taste made cupcakes extra amazing. But they turned a place like Osiris into a mishmash of olfactory sensations —not all of them pleasant. The scents of dozens of perfumes and aftershaves invaded my nostrils, intermingled with the smell of booze, sweat, and musk.

Pete passed my drink over, and I gulped down a quick sip, trying to block out the other smells. The flavor exploded on my tongue, and I smiled.

The burly man chuckled. "You like it?"

I nodded enthusiastically and turned to watch the crowd in the bar.

Grace was dropping off a tray of drinks at a table in the back. When she glanced up and caught sight of me, her eyes widened. She beelined over, pulling me into an enthusiastic hug.

We were work friends because Grace had decided we would be. Not that I'd had any objections, but if it'd been left up to me, we probably would've only said a few words to each other. I was naturally somewhat of a loner, and nine years of marriage to Kyle had only exacerbated that. But Grace, who started at Osiris a few months before I did, wasn't bothered by my quiet demeanor one bit. Her bubbly personality more than made up for my shyness.

"Welcome back to the land of the living!" She grinned at me when she finally released me. Then her dark eyes went wide as she looked me up and down. "Woah. Willow, what the hell?"

"What? What is it?" My stomach dropped. No one else had noticed anything strange about me. What had she seen?

Grace wolf whistled. Her full lips pursed as she examined me, her nose ring flashing in the dim colored lights of the bar. She had dark skin and a short afro that hugged her head, and her eyes always sparkled with a hint of mischief.

"You look different!" she exclaimed, turning my body from side to side as she continued her perusal.

I stepped back, slipping out of her grasp with an uncomfortable shrug. "Um, no, I don't think so."

"You *do*," she insisted. "Holy hell, you *so* do. Your skin looks incredible, and you're fucking rocking that dress. You look amazing! Good lord, every guy in the room is checking you out. Hell, I'm checking you out!"

"Oh. Well, thanks." I groped on the bar for my drink, bringing it to my lips with a shaky hand. At least she hadn't noticed anything *way* off about me. Like fangs poking out of my mouth or something. "You look great too," I added, in a desperate attempt to distract her.

I should've known it was pointless. Grace had latched onto her discovery like a pit bull clinging to its favorite chew toy.

"I can't get over it! You're, like, glowing or something." Her eyes narrowed. "Oh my God. *Did you get laid*?"

Heat flooded my cheeks, and even though the bar was noisy, I shushed her quickly.

"No!" Then I hesitated. That was probably the safest explanation for all this, and it would definitely distract her. "All right, maybe."

Grace grinned triumphantly. I tried to slip past her toward the bathrooms, but she blocked my path.

"Nuh-uh. You're not getting away that easily. Who is this guy? Tell me about him!"

I froze, momentarily tongue-tied. I didn't have a lie prepared for this.

"Um… Well, he's really tall." An image of the nameless man

with dark hair flashed through my mind. "Six-foot-four maybe. With broad shoulders." Jerrett's piercing blue eyes hovered in my memory, nearly stealing my breath. "Blue eyes." Sol's kind face followed, with his serious expression and messy golden hair. "Wavy blond hair, and a little dimple in his chin."

"Day-um! Go, Willow!" Grace raised her eyebrows, smirking at me. "So does he have a brother?"

I swallowed. *No, he doesn't have a brother, he has two.*

And the man I'd just described was an amalgamation of all of them. How did I remember their faces so well? I hadn't spent more than a few minutes with them.

"Uh... I don't know. I'll ask him for you," I muttered, staring down into my drink like there was a prize at the bottom.

"Well, either way, I'm glad you're getting some hot man action. 'Bout time!" Grace elbowed up to the bar next to me and flagged down Pete. "Hey, Petey! Two shots of Patron. My girl needs to celebrate!"

Pete grinned and slid the drinks down the bar. Grace toasted me before tossing hers back like a pro. I mirrored her action more slowly, unable to keep the grimace off my face as the alcohol burned its way down my throat. Everything about it was more intense with vampire senses, and I coughed as I set the empty glass on the bar.

Grace winked at me then slipped away to check on her tables.

As the burn in my throat eased, it was replaced by a deeper ache in my chest. I rubbed my sternum absently, hardly noticing how the guy next to me followed the movement of my hand before his gaze slid lower, ogling my breasts.

As sweet as Grace was to be excited for me, none of what she thought we were celebrating had actually happened. I hadn't had a hot hookup with some amazing guy—I'd been attacked by a supernatural monster, turned into a vampire by three mysterious brothers, and then unceremoniously tossed out on my ass.

If anything, I was drinking to forget.

With that thought in mind, I nodded to Pete for another shot. Then another.

I hadn't drunk this heavily since the night I'd decided to ask Kyle for a divorce. Given my lightweight status, I should've been seeing double by the time I plunked down the third empty shot glass. But although I felt buzzy and light, I wasn't falling off my chair yet. Maybe being a vampire affected how I metabolized alcohol too. I hadn't read anything about that in my online research.

A little while later, Grace went on break and came looking for me again. Maybe she'd noticed me inexplicably moping into my drink, because she hauled me off the stool I'd settled onto and dragged me over to the dance floor.

This was the part of the night I usually dreaded most as a cocktail waitress. The crowd was getting looser, sloppier, and more people pressed themselves onto the dance floor that dominated one corner of the large space. When I was trying to work, it was sort of a pain in the ass. More spilled drinks, more wandering hands.

But as a slightly tipsy bar patron?

It was freaking amazing.

Grace nodded encouragingly as I moved along with the song blaring through the speakers. I couldn't even remember the last time I'd danced in public. But the throbbing beat of the music, the low, flickering lights, the gyrating bodies and rapid thrum of dozens of heartbeats around me—it all swept me away, pulling me out of myself, erasing my worries and fears.

I hadn't gotten drunk from the alcohol. But I was drunk on this.

Twisting and whirling, I lost sight of Grace. But I didn't care. Other bodies moved in to fill the space around me, and I let myself be swept away.

There was plenty of time to return to reality later.

After all, I had all the time in the world now.

12

MALCOLM

I WATCHED her from the shadows of the bar. No one noticed me at the edge of the crowd in the darkness. She certainly didn't.

But everyone noticed her.

I wasn't the only one staring. In a room full of beautiful women, this dark-haired goddess stood out like a fallen star. Her beauty and energy cast a glow on everyone around her.

She's perfect.

Lust poured toward her from the human men in the room, though she seemed to be totally unaware of it. Her head was thrown back, her eyes nearly closed as her hips moved rhythmically, her delicate hands twisting through the air.

I remembered what it'd been like for me back at the start. It was like being reborn, seeing the world I thought I knew through a fresh set of eyes and experiencing every sensation for the first time. For a while, I'd been satisfied living in wanton carnality, indulging the whims of my flesh. Like her, I'd sought out throngs of people, not even aware I was doing it. Being surrounded by bodies with fresh blood pumping through them had given me a high like no alcohol or drug ever could.

A man stepped up to her, his grasping hands latching onto her hips as he matched his rhythm to hers. I watched them move together with an unpleasant mixture of jealousy and arousal twisting in my stomach. The fucking lech didn't deserve to touch her body like that. He didn't know the value of the gem he was pawing at.

Willow.

That was her name.

Sol had told it to me, a quiet pride in his voice as he spoke. As if she'd given him some kind of gift by telling him her name first.

But she *had,* and jealousy burned through me to think he'd known it before I did. Why hadn't I asked her name? Told her mine? We'd been alone together in that room when I fed her, our gazes locked together—and yet I hadn't found the mental acuity to say more than two words to her.

And now I watched her from the shadows like a goddamned stalker.

A fresh wave of self-loathing washed through me. But even that wasn't enough to pull my attention away from the woman.

She was changing.

I barely knew her, had never spoken to her before my brothers and I turned her, but the shift in her was obvious anyway. I recognized it from the other new vampires I'd seen over the years. The transformation from human to vampire was like being put under a magnifying glass—it heightened and sharpened the traits that were already there. Leches became more lustful, risk-takers became daredevils, and the wise became sage-like.

Willow Tate was a woman who craved freedom, and as I

watched from my hidden vantage point, she began to take it. There was a wildness and inhibition in her now that called to me, begging me to let go and join her.

I'd always lived with restraint. As a young man trying to make my fortune in the American colonies, I'd had to. I'd had grand plans for my life, before all those hopes had been ripped away from me.

The careful control I held over myself became even more pronounced after I moved on from the hedonism of my first months as a vampire. And it'd only grown stronger over the years.

Recklessness is a luxury of the stupid.

But now, for the first time in many, many years, I was acting both stupid and reckless.

I cursed myself for my weakness as I tore my gaze away from the soft curves of Willow's body. I'd grown hard just watching her. It wasn't like me to be this bewitched by a woman. My plan to send her away and erase her from my mind had proved a catastrophic failure. The harder I tried to forget her, the more deeply every aspect of this woman embedded itself in my memory.

Sol and Jerrett didn't know I was here, and I planned to keep it that way. Jerrett would call me a hypocrite if he found out, and I'd have no rebuttal for him. I was a hypocrite. And an idiot.

We still hunted the shades that roamed the city, and I was convinced by now that Jerrett was correct—there was more than one of those creatures stalking the streets.

But every moment of the past week not dedicated to the hunt had been spent following Willow.

It had started when I tailed the car I sent her home in the night we'd said goodbye. Despite my brothers' accusations of callousness, I'd been wracked with guilt for sending her away like that. Her glittering hazel eyes had been full of turmoil as I'd put her in the car. I had told myself my only intention was to make sure she got home all right, to ensure she didn't lose control and attack the driver.

But somehow, against all my will and better judgment, I had *kept* watching her. Every evening for the past week, she'd taken down the blanket covering her window and gazed out at the street below, a look of such intense longing on her face it made me ache.

My flimsy excuse of following her for her protection was running out. She'd obviously handled the transition incredibly well. Some people took much longer to adjust to the onslaught of new senses and sensations. Some lost themselves to their primal instincts for time. But Willow's recovery was faster than any I'd seen. She looked right at home in her newly vampiric skin.

Skin that was currently being salivated on by a Wall Street jackass with a bad spray tan and too much gel in his hair.

My lips curled back, my fangs dropping as unreasonable rage consumed me.

Mine.

The thought had barely registered before I was slipping out of the shadows, maneuvering quickly through the throng of bodies like a ghost. I circled around behind the two of them, careful to stay out of Willow's periphery. Then I dropped a heavy hand on the man's shoulder.

He glanced up, his half-lidded eyes foggy from drink. They widened as he took in the expression on my face. The man was smarter than he looked—he recognized a predator when he saw one. Backing away from Willow, he slithered into the crowd with his tail between his legs. She was so lost in the beat she didn't even notice, brushing her ass against me as she danced.

My heart froze.

Against my will, as if someone else controlled the movements of my body, I put my hands on her hips, caressing her flesh gently through the silky fabric of her dress.

The rational part of my brain screamed at me to stop. This was too fucking dangerous. Worse than sneaking around behind my brothers' backs. Worse than watching her in secret. Willow could turn around at any moment and discover who I was. She was a newly made vampire, with acute senses and enhanced speed and strength. It was only a matter of time before she recognized my scent.

But while those alarms rang in my mind, her body pressed against me, warm and sweet and impossible to deny. I wrapped my arms tighter around her and buried my face in her hair—as though indulging in my craving would somehow help me vanquish it.

Her body softened, becoming almost boneless in my arms as the smallest sound of pleasure fell from her lips.

We moved together in perfect harmony, as if the very rhythm of our souls intertwined. Her perfect ass ground against my cock, both intensifying and relieving the ache in my balls. I pressed into her harder, wrapping my arms more tightly around her.

Then she began to turn her head, and I froze.

Regret and shame barreled into me with the force of a speeding car.

What am I doing? Am I a goddamned animal? Can I not control my impulses at all?

I hadn't acted this reckless since the days after I was turned, when rage and resentment had burned hot in my veins, eradicating all rational thought.

Her body began to follow the movement of her head, but before she could turn around and catch sight of me, I tore myself away, disappearing into the mass of writhing bodies.

I stalked outside and slid back into the shadows on the street. My fist lashed out, shattering a car window as I passed. Jerrett had been right about that, at least; it did make me feel marginally better.

Never again, Malcolm. Fuck. Never again. This ends here.

13

WILLOW

I STUMBLED BACKWARD as the man dancing behind me disappeared suddenly. Disoriented, I looked around, but he was nowhere to be seen.

What the hell? What an asshole.

I'd been having an amazing time, and I thought he had been too.

It was strange. He hadn't been much of a dance partner at first, his movements a little clumsy and out of rhythm. It hadn't bothered me much—I was so swept up in the music I would've danced with a coat rack.

But then, out of nowhere, he'd turned up the heat several dozen notches.

His hands became more confident and demanding, roaming my body with a possessiveness I was startled to find I liked. He'd touched me as if I belonged to him, and I hadn't found myself inclined to argue one bit. My nerve endings still prickled where his warm palms had splayed across the fabric of my dress.

I stopped dancing and stared stupidly around the dance floor, an island of stillness in a sea of movement. I didn't see the guy. Not that I knew for sure who he was, since I'd never gotten a glimpse of his face. But I didn't see anyone who looked like I imagined he did.

My stomach sank. I shoved my way through the crowd, no longer in the mood for any of this. The high I'd ridden for the past few hours was fading, and I was about to make an unpleasant crash landing back on earth.

Get a grip, Willow. You're losing it.

I shook my head, irritation at myself souring my stomach. Even though I knew it was just some random frat guy out with his buddies, I had found myself imagining it was one of the brothers dancing with me. Especially when his dancing improved, and he began to handle my body with such ease and power. I'd gotten lost in images of rich brown eyes, bright blue eyes, and entrancing green eyes—imagined the way each of them smelled, the strength and grace of their large bodies. I'd even thought I caught the scent of leather for a brief moment.

Ugh. This does not count as getting a grip, you dummy.

Frustrated tears burned my eyes as I tried to escape the suddenly claustrophobic confines of the bar. The scents, the sounds, the press of bodies… It was all suddenly too much.

The vampire brothers had lied. I couldn't go back to my old life. Even the small parts I'd hoped might be left to me were disintegrating before my eyes. The changes I'd gone through because of them had affected me on a much deeper level than simply making me allergic to sunlight.

Who am *I now? I wasn't this person a week ago.*

I'd never had a one-night stand, never picked up a guy in a bar and brought him home without even learning his name. I'd only slept with two men in my life, and I'd been certain I was in love with each of them at the time.

But tonight, I'd been on the verge of spinning around, kissing the hell out of the guy dancing behind me, and begging him to take me home. Or, shit, just to the alley out back. Burning tension had built in my body, stoked even higher by his purposeful caresses, and I'd been desperate for some kind of release.

I still was.

But all these new feelings and experiences were coming at me too fast, leaving me reeling. Which woman was I? The one who'd had boring sex with the same guy for the past nine years and hadn't even been able to face the idea of going on a date with a new man? Or the one who'd almost dragged a stranger into an alley and ripped off his clothes?

Could I be both?

The cool air hit my face as I stepped outside, sending goose bumps across my exposed skin. But it felt good. It woke me up and shocked me the rest of the way back to sober. I hesitated by the door, shifting to the side as a group of drunk bar-hoppers pushed past me.

Damn it. I hadn't told Grace I was leaving.

Bracing myself, I slipped back into the onslaught of scents and sounds. A few minutes of searching revealed Grace flirting shamelessly with a tableful of blond-haired Wall Street clones. One of them gave me a funny look as I approached, but I ignored him, waiting until Grace finished taking their order to tap her on the shoulder.

She turned to me, her cat-eye makeup flawless despite the late hour. Grace always looked as fresh at the end of her shift as she did at the beginning, something I'd never mastered.

"Hey!" She beamed as we walked back toward the bar

together. "Sorry I lost you for a bit there. I had to go back to work, but I didn't want to interrupt." She winked bawdily. "You looked like you were having fun."

"Yeah." I smiled tiredly. "I was."

Grace pulled me into another hug. "Let's do it again sometime. You have to let me take you out!"

"Sure, I'd like that. See you later, Grace."

"Bye, hot stuff! Enjoy your fine piece of man."

She slapped me on the butt as I turned to leave, and when I looked back in shock, she raised her eyebrows and stuck her tongue out. Despite the several impending emotional freak-outs hanging over me, I grinned at her as I walked away.

Grace was a great person. I only wished it hadn't taken me becoming a vampire to really start to bond with her. If I'd just been a little bit braver when I was a human and reached out to her then, we might have become real friends instead of just work buddies.

Do vampires even have friends?

Sol, Jerrett, and the dark-haired one didn't look anything alike, but they called themselves brothers. I needed to do what they'd done and find my own group, my own clan. But how the hell was I supposed to do that? I didn't know any other stupid vampires besides them.

And they'd been very specific in their instructions not to let anyone know what I was.

Stepping out onto the sidewalk again, I decided to walk home. I was restless and antsy, my thoughts too loud for me to go back to my silent, stifling apartment yet. It felt good to be outside, and besides, wasn't I a creature of the night now? Shouldn't the things that lurked in dark shadows fear *me*?

I set off at a quick pace down the sidewalk, testing out my

new senses of hearing and smell as I walked. Odors occasionally became overwhelming, especially when I passed by a strip of bars with their doors propped open, but I found that I could dampen the sense if I needed to, bringing it down to nearly human levels.

My sense of hearing was the same. Almost like I had a little volume dial in my brain I could turn up or down. If I turned the knob as far as it would go, I could pick up every footstep of the people walking near me, even on the other side of the street. I could hear glasses clinking inside the bars I passed. And *dozens* of overlapping conversations around me.

It was like a mega-dose of humanity, served directly into my eardrums. Thankfully, before it could completely overwhelm me, I passed into a quieter neighborhood.

Now I picked up different sounds. Trash can lids banging, small rodents skittering through dark alleys, leaves rustling, and...

Footsteps?

My pace slowed as my heart rate picked up. I pricked my ears, listening intently.

A few blocks from my apartment, a familiar scent hit my nose. Smoke and cloves. I recognized that smell; it belonged to one of the vampires who'd turned me. He was following me. I was sure of it.

Swinging around, I crossed my arms over my chest, trying to look cocky and annoyed rather than slightly relieved.

"Hey! You can come out!" I called, craning my neck to peer into the shadows. "I know you're there."

Half a block away, a figure emerged from the darkness.

But it wasn't a vampire.

14

WILLOW

"OH SHIT..."

The words fell from my lips as my muscles bunched in fear.

Another shadow creature lurched toward me, barely visible in the dim light. Was it the same one that had attacked me a week ago? I couldn't tell, and there were no distinguishing marks on the mass of darkness and sharp claws.

Something tickled my gums, and I realized my fangs had dropped—my vampiric fight-or-flight impulse kicking in.

It hadn't gone well last time I'd chosen "fight," but this time I was no longer a weak and helpless human. I was a supernatural creature with enhanced senses and abilities. I may not look like much, but I was faster and stronger than I'd been then. And now was my chance to exact revenge on this thing for ruining my life.

Or die trying.

Not giving myself too long to linger on that dark thought, or my full motivations for acting so recklessly, I lunged to my left.

A discarded length of two-by-four lay on the sidewalk. I

snatched it up and pivoted, swinging the piece of wood like a club.

It collided with the shade's shoulder, the blow so strong it cracked the wood in half and made the creature stumble.

Before it could regain its footing, I darted forward again. Blood rushed in my ears, and my lips curled back in a mask of rage as I rammed the jagged end of the wood into the monster's midsection.

It gave an echoing screech and shuffled backward, something black and thick oozing from its middle.

I dodged easily when it lunged at me, then I darted forward to land another strike on what looked like its arm. Its appearance was so dark and ephemeral, it was hard to tell.

Yep. It's an arm.

The claw tipped hand attached to that arm whipped out, punching me in the sternum and sending me flying backward. I skidded on the sidewalk, my chest burning where the claws had nicked me, and the back of my legs and arms stinging with road rash.

I'd managed to keep hold of my weapon, at least, and I leapt forward again, charging toward the shade faster than I ever could've run as a human.

Not that it did much good.

I swung for the creature, landing what should've been a direct hit. But this time, my chunk of two-by-four passed through its body as if the thing really was made of smoke.

What the hell? No wonder I'd thought the thing had no mass the first time I saw it. It could become incorporeal.

Whatever trick the shade had pulled, it didn't last long. The momentum of my swing pulled me off balance, and as I spun around, a very solid hand grabbed my upper arm from behind.

The shade drove me forward, slamming me into the wall of an empty office building. Its other hand pressed against the side of my head, mashing my cheek into the rough brick.

Puffs of fetid air blew into my face, and I swung wildly with my makeshift club, but I couldn't hit anything from this angle.

Another scent hit my nose. Smoke and cloves. I hadn't imagined it before.

Leather and musk wafted through the air too, followed by something warm and spicy.

The shade's claws pierced the skin at the back of my neck just as movement flashed in the corner of my vision.

The tall, cranky man stepped from the shadows. "Let her go, shade. I won't warn you again."

The creature hissed, turning away from me but keeping my body pressed against the wall. I craned my neck to glance behind me as Jerrett and Sol appeared from opposite ends of the street.

"What the fuck, Mal?" Jerrett called. "I knew you were fucking following her!"

The shade hissed, drawing the men's attention again. Malcolm lunged toward it, moving so fast he was nearly a blur. He grabbed the creature and spun it away from me, hurling it to the ground.

"*Me?*" he shouted at Jerrett as they both leapt after the shade. They landed in a crouch, and Jerrett pulled a silver dagger from his boot while the tall man—Mal?—pinned the creature down. "What are *you* doing here? You just happened to be out for a stroll in this neighborhood?"

"Yeah, maybe I fucking did! You don't know my life!"

Jerrett slammed his blade down into the monster's chest—or tried to, anyway. But the dagger passed right through it as it shifted into nothingness again.

The thing scrambled away while they grasped at it uselessly.

"Goddamnit!"

"Don't let it get away!"

"Jerrett! Here!"

Sol's voice drew my attention. I sucked in a terrified breath as Jerrett spun… and threw the dagger straight at him.

But the blond man didn't hesitate. He didn't even flinch. Snatching the blade out of the air, he slashed at the shade as it passed by him, gouging deep into its side. The creature shrieked again, a furious, pained sound.

"Hey, don't think we're not wondering why you're here too, pretty boy!" Jerrett called, as he and Mal sprinted toward Sol and the injured shade.

Sol darted forward, ducking under the shade's arm and lashing out with the dagger again. "Has it ever occurred to you that I was just following *you two*?"

"Not for one goddamned second," Mal grunted.

He slammed into the shade and wrestled its thick arms behind its back, but the creature slipped into shadow again and slithered out of his grip. It spun and lashed out, catching Mal across the face. Three deep cuts opened up on his cheek.

"Fuck! Mal?" Jerrett called.

"It's nothing. I'm all right!"

"Jerrett. It's running!"

Sol's cry pulled my focus from the blood on Mal's face. I wasn't sure how the blind man had known, but he was right. The creature was moving swiftly away into the night.

No way! You don't get off that easy, you coward.

I pushed away from the wall, launching myself after the shade and throwing myself on its back. Either I caught it by surprise, or it didn't think I was much of a threat, because it didn't go incorporeal on me.

"Holy fuck! Damn, girl!"

Jerrett let out a low whistle and I heard someone else—the man called Mal, probably—curse under his breath. The shade hurled me off its back just as the brothers reached us. For the second time in one evening, I skidded across rough cement like a baseball player sliding for home.

When I finally ground to a stop, I rolled over. A grotesque ripping sound filled the air, and a second later, Jerrett held one of the creature's arms aloft.

A keening cry pierced the night. The shade went incorporeal and kept fading away until I could hardly see it. A faint, ghostly shadow flickered up the dimly lit street and vanished.

My gaze shot back to Jerrett, who held the shade's thick, black arm in his hands. As I watched, the limb shriveled, losing mass and color. A moment later, it had become spindly and gray, almost resembling mummified flesh.

Jerrett slapped the dry, bony limb against his open palm. He looked up to meet his brothers' eyes.

"Well. This is fucking great."

15

JERRETT

MAL'S LIPS pressed into a harsh line as he stared at the desiccated arm I held.

Then he turned and extended a hand down to Willow. Her dress had ridden up a little when she skidded, exposing most of her smooth, lightly tanned thighs. Damn, she had killer legs. And had she fought the shade in those heels?

What do you know? Sexy and *a badass.*

But as soon as she was on her feet, Mal had both hands on her shoulders, pushing her against the wall of a tall building nearby. Her back hit the brick with a smack, and she stared up at him in shock.

"What the fuck were you thinking?" my brother raged. He put his face inches from hers, fear making his voice harsh. "Walking home alone *again*? Taking that thing on by yourself?" He shook her. "Do you have some kind of damn death wish? Vampires are immortal, not invincible. We can still die. Don't you understand that?"

Willow blinked rapidly, her large hazel eyes glistening in the dim streetlights. A shadow of sadness flickered over her face, and my blood froze.

Shit. She knew exactly what the fuck she was doing.

Guilt slithered up my spine like a snake. We had turned her and then set her loose in the world, and she'd run toward death with open arms.

But the spark of life in her was too strong to be extinguished.

Her jaw took on a stubborn set. The glassiness in her eyes faded, and she smacked Mal in the chest with both hands. Hard.

"Why would I know that? You never *told me anything*! You just kicked me out and left me to fend for myself."

"Because I thought you had more sense than to go looking for a fight with a goddamned undead supernatural!"

Willow strained against Mal's grip, closing the distance between their faces and going nose-to-nose with him. "I didn't 'go looking' for a fight! That thing followed me. And what the hell are *you* all doing following me anyway? I thought the whole point was that you never wanted to see me—" She stopped suddenly, her nostrils flaring as she inhaled deeply. Her voice was low when she spoke again. "Oh my God… It was you. At Osiris. I recognize that scent. You… you were there. You danced with me."

Sol's shoulder brushed mine as he came to stand beside me, cocking his head. "What's this now?"

Mal shot a look at us, guilt flashing in his eyes.

Holy fuck. That sneaky motherfucker!

And here I thought I'd been breaking the rules by checking in on Willow occasionally. This dickhead was off creeping into bars and grinding up on her like a horny teenager.

My brother looked back at Willow but didn't answer her question. "You should be glad we were all here tonight. Things could've gone very differently if we weren't."

She shoved him again. Damn, she was a fucking firecracker. "I didn't ask for your help! So leave me alone! Haven't you done enough?"

Mal's chest heaved as he glared at her. "We saved your life."

"You turned me into a vampire!"

"Hey! Shut the fuck up or I'm calling the cops! Do your weird-ass role-playing somewhere else!"

The shout from a nearby apartment building drew all of our attention. A window slammed shut on the third floor.

"We need to get out of here," Sol murmured.

I scrubbed a hand down my face. "Right. Jesus."

We were never this sloppy on a hunt. Willow had us all completely off our game.

"Yeah, Mal," I drawled. "Do your kinky role-playing somewhere else."

He took a step back, keeping his voice at a low volume this time. "He said 'weird,' not 'kinky.'"

The second she had a little more space, Willow sucked in a deep breath. As she released it, the anger and tension drained from her body, and she reached tentatively toward Mal. One side of his face was covered in blood.

"Are you… all right?"

Mal's expression softened. "Yes. I'm fine. We heal quickly." He wiped his forearm over his cheek, showing her the already closed wounds. "Are you all right?"

Willow nodded slowly, her eyes going out of focus like she was doing an internal check of her injuries. "Yeah. Some scrapes and bruises, and—"

She glanced down. The front of her dress had several long claw marks across it. The tears in the fabric didn't expose anything too risqué, but she put her hand over them anyway.

"I'm fine."

A smirk tilted my lips. The little black dress hugged her curves in an understated but sexy way. I didn't mind the rips in it either, although I hated how she'd gotten them.

Mal's face darkened with concern, and he skimmed his hands lightly down her arms.

He really is a sneaky motherfucker. First with the dancing, now with the checking her for wounds?

I cleared my throat loudly.

"Much as I hate to interrupt your foreplay"—I held up the arm I'd torn from the shade, making it wave at them—"there are a few important things we need to discuss."

Sol reached over to take the arm from me. His fingers traced over the dried-out skin, and he frowned. "There are markings on this."

"Really?" I looked at the gray-skinned arm again as Mal and Willow came closer to peer over my shoulder.

On closer inspection, I realized Sol was right. The arm was decorated with a pattern of scars.

"Runes of some sort," my youngest brother added.

Mal's brow furrowed. "Like the ones the shade was trying to carve into Willow the night we saved her?"

"It seems likely."

"So this second attack on her wasn't a coincidence."

"What? What does that mean?" Willow's gaze darted among the three of us.

"We've been hunting this thing for a while," I explained, catching Mal's gaze. "It's a shade, an undead creature. And actually, I should say we've been hunting these *things*, plural—because there are definitely more than one."

"Okay. But what about the runes?"

I bit my lip ring. "This hunt has been difficult because we couldn't figure out what these things were after or why they were in the city. But I'm starting to get a pretty clear idea of what they want."

"And?" she asked, her voice wavering slightly. "What are they looking for?"

She was smart enough to know the answer before I said it, but I knew she needed to hear it out loud.

"You."

Willow's pupils dilated, and her throat worked as she swallowed. "What? Why? I'm just an ordinary human! At least, I was when it attacked me the first time. I'm a nobody from Ohio. Why would it want me?"

I tipped my head, eyeing her. "Yeah, you were human. But I don't think you were ever ordinary."

Grabbing the shade's limb back from Sol, I stepped toward Willow. I grasped her upper arm and raised it slightly. Her skin was soft as silk under my touch, and a riot of goose bumps broke out on her flesh at my touch. I heard her breath hitch and had to fight not to tighten my grip on her. She smelled just as fucking good as I remembered.

Willow winced as I placed the shade's severed arm next to hers for comparison. The faint white scars on her arm stood out in the dim light—and they were nearly identical to the markings on the gray, dried skin of the shade.

"See?" I looked up into her eyes, twin green-gold pools that shone in the darkness. "You should've healed completely when we turned you, but these scars remained. Those wounds had some kind of magical property. You've been marked."

Sol stepped forward. "And it wasn't a coincidence you were attacked twice. You were being targeted. But the good news is, now that we know, we can use it to our advantage. You can help us discover exactly what these shades are and what they want with you."

Mal and I both nodded, but the spark of anger lit in Willow's eyes again.

"*Help* you? Why would I do that? Didn't we just establish that you pretty much wrecked my life?"

"We can help you too, Willow."

Sol's voice was soothing, and I rolled my eyes. *You don't soothe a firecracker into not exploding.*

"No!" Willow held her hands up. "I'm sorry, but no! I'm done with all of this. I want off this insane ride. I just want to go back to whatever job I have left, keep my head down, and try to rebuild some semblance of a life for myself."

Mal glowered at her. "Do you truly think you can fight off the shades yourself? You are being hunted. Stalked by undead supernaturals. They're going to keep attacking you, maybe as a group next time. What will you do then? This one nearly killed you, and he was alone. I told you. Just because you're stronger now, that doesn't make you invincible."

Her sweet face paled, but her chin lifted. "I'll figure something out. I don't want your help!"

Mal opened his mouth to argue, but I cut him off with a look. She wasn't stupid. She'd make the right choice. She just needed a minute to come to terms with it.

The best way to handle a firecracker is to get to a safe distance and let it combust on its own.

"You heard her, brothers." I dipped my head at Willow in a mock bow. "The lady wants to be left alone. Let's go."

I turned sharply and headed up the street. Mal and Sol followed close on my heels.

We made it a few blocks before a yell of frustration echoed in the darkness behind us. A few moments later, I heard her soft footsteps padding toward us, moving quickly to catch up.

A grin tugged at the corner of my lips.

Good call, sweetheart.

16

WILLOW

I WATCHED the three brothers walk away under the light of the street lamps. A battle raged in my chest as I stood frozen in place. The smart voice in my head was telling me to go home and lay low, to avoid all of this. To stay the hell away from vampires, shadow creatures, and anything else that went bump in the night. To go back to work at the bar, maybe take Grace up on her offer to go clubbing sometime, and just generally act like none of this had happened.

Or maybe that *wasn't* the smart voice in my head. Maybe that was the dumb, scared, stubborn voice.

Mal was right. As much as it pained me to admit it, I probably couldn't take on one of those shades by myself. They were too strong, too *magical.* If a single one attacked me, the best I could do was escape. If I was ambushed by a group? I'd be dead.

And as foolhardy and reckless as I'd acted thirty minutes ago, I really didn't want to die.

If I tried to get through this on my own, chances were

extremely high the shades would get what they wanted from me. Whatever that was.

But would I be safer with the brothers?

There were no guarantees. I hardly knew the three men. But somehow, they'd become the only lifeline I had in this strange new world. Helpless anger and frustration welled in my chest, and I tipped my head back and screamed into the night.

"That's it! I'm calling the fucking cops, lady!"

The irate man from earlier leaned out of his window, waving his cell phone at me.

Grimacing, I set off quickly down the street before he could make good on his promise. Worry still gnawed at my stomach, but surprisingly, my chest felt a bit lighter. As much as I wanted to blame the vampires for all this, I knew it wasn't their fault. I'd been attacked by the shadow creature first, and by the time the brothers found me, they'd had only two choices—let me die, or turn me.

Truthfully, I was glad they'd chosen the latter.

Mal, Jerrett, and Sol came into view ahead of me a few blocks over, weaving through the shadows like ghosts.

A ripple of fear passed through me at the unearthly sight of them.

Vampires are real.

So are shades. The undead.

Were there other kinds of supernatural creatures out there? Things worse than shades? More dangerous than vampires? My entire worldview had been turned on its head, and that opened the door to terrifying new possibilities. I might be a vampire now, but that didn't mean I was automatically equipped to deal with the supernatural world. I was barely getting the hang of my new abilities—hell, I didn't even know what all of them were.

I was out of my depth, big time.

"So… what now?" I asked quietly, falling into step with the three men. The one named Mal didn't even glance at me, but Sol smiled in my direction.

"We need to identify what the shades are after. And we need to keep you safe. We'll take you back home with us."

"Where you should've stayed from day one." Jerrett threw a pointed look at Mal.

"You know why I didn't want that," Mal answered. "I'm still not sure it's a good idea, but we have no choice."

"Are there… other monsters out there?" I swallowed. "Worse ones?"

Sol's fingers brushed my hand. He lifted it and tucked it gently into the crook of his elbow, a surprisingly gentlemanly gesture. It felt strange being led down the street by a man who couldn't see, but then again, I'd just witnessed him pluck a knife out of the air. I supposed I didn't need to worry about him steering me into a tree or anything.

"There are all kinds of supernaturals in the world, Willow. Not all are evil, though many are dangerous. Humans are ignorant of their existence, for the most part. Supernaturals live in shadows, and people don't *want* to believe. They never notice what's right under their noses, do they?"

I couldn't argue with that. I'd always thought of myself as pretty perceptive, but becoming a vampire was like having a veil lifted from my eyes. I could truly *see* now. I could smell now. I could feel everything. It was a little like the first time I'd watched a 3-D movie, only more nausea inducing.

"Are there other supernaturals here in New York?"

"Yes, some. Loners and outcasts, mostly. Entire civilizations of supernaturals exist in places humans can't discover. Only a small number of us chose to live among humanity."

"So, which are you guys—loners or outcasts?" I asked. I thought it was a fair question, but Mal stopped in his tracks ahead of us to glower at me. Jerrett snorted, and Sol chuckled.

I met the tall man's dark glare with a lifted chin. If I was going to be stuck with them for the foreseeable future, he needed to know I wasn't scared of him.

Or at least, he needed to *think* I wasn't scared of him.

"We're hunters by choice." Mal turned around and resumed walking. "We live without a clan so we can watch over the world. Our sworn duty is to keep it safe from evil beings and rogue supernaturals who would attack humans—or even other supernaturals. There are dangerous creatures out there that need to be kept in line." He paused, then added, "Someone has to do it, don't they?"

The tone of his voice changed as he spoke those last words, becoming hard and bitter. I was curious what he'd meant by that, but I didn't press. He didn't seem to be in the mood to answer questions.

"We made our base in New York because the city is a constant draw to supernaturals," Sol said "There's so much life and activity here—and with the size and diversity of the population, it's easier for nonhumans to blend in."

"That makes sense," I murmured. I'd seen a few people on the subway I would have no problem believing weren't entirely human.

"We've been tracking the shades for a while." Jerrett swung the shriveled arm like a baseball bat, earning him a grunt of disapproval from Mal. "It's becoming pretty obvious that they're working together with some kind of end goal in mind. They have a purpose. A task to complete. And they're not going to rest until they do."

"And what do they want with me?"

"Yeah… that part I don't know yet. But they definitely want you, sweetheart. I mean, shit—can't say I blame them for that." He winked at me, his bright blue eyes glittering like stars.

I was glad the darkness hid my blush, but I swore Sol could feel the heat rising to my cheeks, because he chuckled softly beside me.

Trying to get the conversation back on track, I cleared my throat. "So a bunch of undead supernaturals are after me for some unknown reason. What am I supposed to do about that? How do I stay safe?"

Mal shot another look over his shoulder, his expression serious.

"The first thing we need to do is train you."

17

MALCOLM

I RAPPED my knuckles sharply on the door of the guest bedroom.

"Uh, hold on! I'm almost ready!"

Panic sounded in Willow's voice, and I had a sudden vision of her rushing around the room as she scrambled to finish dressing. I could imagine her tugging a shirt over her head and pulling it down to cover the milky softness of her breasts, the smooth plane of her stomach, the swell of her hips.

Clenching my jaw, I forced those images from my mind. This was exactly why I'd tried to send her away, as misguided as that attempt may have been. Jerrett would never let me live my weakness down.

It's not entirely fair, I groused to myself. *He followed her in secret too.*

The only difference was, such a flagrant violation of the rules wasn't at all out of character for Jerrett—but it was for me.

The door swung open, and Willow greeted me. Her hair was slightly disheveled, and she tugged down the hem of her loose white t-shirt. It seemed my imagination hadn't been far off after all.

"Is this okay?" She gestured to her t-shirt and the tight, stretchy black pants she wore.

"Yes. That's fine. You just need something you can move in."

Dragging my gaze away from her body, I canted my head down the hallway. She pulled her door shut and fell into step beside me.

It'd been nearly dawn by the time we arrived home after our encounter with the shade, and Willow had clearly been exhausted. She needed a good day's sleep, so I'd had Yuliya make up a guest bedroom for her—though *not* the same room she'd stayed in last time.

I'd botched the girl's transformation just about as badly as was possible, and I wanted to start Willow's stay with us on the right foot. Putting her in the same room where she'd once woken up terrified, alone, and strapped to a bed didn't seem like the best way to put her at ease.

Truthfully, I wasn't sure anything would do that.

The sun had set a few hours ago. Sol and Jerrett were in the study, working on deciphering the runes on the shade's arm. And as I'd promised last night, I was going to train the girl. My gut roiled every time I considered how much worse the shade's attack on her could have been. If she'd died because we weren't there to protect her, I would never have forgiven myself.

Why do you care so much?

A traitorous voice that sounded suspiciously like Jerrett's whispered insidiously in my head.

Grinding my teeth together, I picked up my pace and led Willow through the large house, as if hoping to outrun my thoughts.

I care what happens to her because she's my responsibility. My brothers and I turned her, and that makes her our charge. That's all.

Willow hurried to keep up with me, her heart slamming against her ribs. She was nervous, though she tried her best to hide it. Her walk was strong and poised, but her pulse gave her away. She didn't trust me, and she was probably right not to.

My predator instincts rippled under my skin as we descended the stairs to the lower level. Her flushed cheeks and wide eyes called to me like a wounded deer calls to a wolf; my muscles shook with the urge to press her up against the wall and show her how little she *should* trust me.

Agreeing to spend more time with her was a mistake. I knew that. The bond between my brothers and the girl was growing, and it was only going to become stronger now that she was living with us.

I hated to admit it, but my own need for her was growing too.

As reckless and insane as it had been to approach her in the bar, I couldn't stop replaying our dance over and over again in my head. I could still remember the warmth and strength of her body as it rocked against mine, the uninhibited joy, passion, and sensuality of her movements.

But the truth was, we needed her in a more practical sense as well. She might be able to help us uncover answers about the shades, why they were attacking, and what they wanted. She was our only lead, and we were her only protection. It was a fair trade.

We reached the basement, and Willow's hazel eyes nearly popped out of her pretty little head when I ushered her inside the training room.

"Oh!" She blinked at her surroundings.

I cocked my head at her, a smile tugging at my lips despite myself. "Just 'oh?'"

Her reaction didn't surprise me. The lower level didn't exactly match the luxurious design of the rest of our house. But this room wasn't meant to be pretty. It was meant to be useful. We didn't need expensive art on the walls or extravagant upholstery here. We just needed a large, unbreakable space.

Somewhere to let our demons out to play.

"What is this place?" She glanced over at me. The specks of gold in her irises shone even under the dingy florescent lighting.

I took off my jacket and threw it to the floor, flexing my shoulders. "This is the best room in the whole house."

Willow scanned her surroundings again doubtfully, as though she might've missed something. There was nothing to miss. A few heavy bags hung from the ceiling in one corner, and a rack of weapons and a small chest of drawers stood against the opposite wall. That was it.

"It is?"

"Yes. This is the training room." I grinned, the excitement of a fight loosening my tense muscles. Sparring always helped calm me down and clear my head.

Willow blanched, biting her plump bottom lip.

"Do I really need training? I mean, it's kind of intuitive, isn't it? I can move a little faster, I'm a little stronger, and I can smell and hear more acutely. Is training neces—"

Before she could finish the word, I had her pinned to the wall with her hand behind her back. Her ass pressed against me as I leaned into her, her cherry and almond scent invading my senses, and I struggled to control my instinctual reaction.

Her body was like a drug I could get high on over and over, but that wasn't the point of this. I couldn't lose focus. I needed to teach her how dangerous it was to underestimate her opponents.

Or to get cocky.

"Yes. Yes it is." My words were a dangerous whisper in her ear. She struggled against my grip, but I didn't let her go yet. "A creature with the same heightened strength and speed as you can easily take the upper hand if you aren't prepared. And those shades are incredibly strong and nearly vampire-fast. You might feel invincible, Willow, but that's only because humans are weak. You have no idea what supernaturals are capable of."

I finally released her, stepping back. She turned around and leaned against the wall—because her legs wouldn't support her weight, I was guessing—but the glare she shot me was fierce.

"Jesus! First on the dance floor, now here. If you grab me like that again, I'll kick your ass!"

"I didn't think you minded it on the dance floor." I raised a mocking brow, ignoring the reaction in my own body at the memory.

Willow's eyes widened. She flushed bright red and looked down, her dark hair falling around her face like a curtain.

"That's not the point," she whispered. "You can't just go around grabbing people without their permission."

Her vulnerability drew out the predator in me, but to my surprise, an even stronger instinct rose in my chest—the need to protect her, to comfort her.

"Wildcat." Stepping closer, I tipped her chin up with the fingers of one hand. Tears glistened in her eyes. My thumb caressed her cheek, the skin soft as rose petals. "There are monsters in this world who wouldn't ask permission to *kill* you, let alone touch you. I'm trying to make sure you can defend yourself from them."

She tugged her lower lip between her teeth, staring at me intently. "And you're not one of them?"

"The monsters?"

Her head dipped slightly, still cupped in my hand.

"No, Willow." I bent down to meet her at eye level, wanting her to see the truth in my eyes. "I try very hard not to be."

"I... I believe you."

A shaky smile broke across her face, and I swore I heard an angelic choir singing. My chest tightened at the sight, an unfamiliar but not unpleasant ache squeezing my heart.

"Good." I cleared my throat and stepped back, giving us both a chance to recover our equilibrium. "I'm going to challenge you in our training because I want you to learn. I want you to have to push yourself, and to feel the adrenaline that comes with danger. But I will never hurt you. I promise."

Willow nodded, stepping away from the wall. I was pleased to note that her legs no longer wobbled. She was strong. Brave.

"Okay. I'm ready."

"You have a lot to learn. Blind determination and balls will usually get you just far enough to get you killed. That shade would've started carving you up in a few seconds if we hadn't found you when we did."

She blew some hair out of her face, frustration clear on her features.

"I was... handling it." At my raised brow, she sighed. "Okay, I wasn't handling it *well*. I want to learn how to move like you guys do. You shift through shadows so quickly. I want to be good at hiding."

Good. She wanted to learn defense before she learned offense. That was the mark of a smart fighter.

"It is a useful skill," I agreed.

I glanced around the room. It was sparse, so there weren't many shadows. But the few pieces of equipment we had were enough. I instructed Willow to watch as I approached one of the heavy bags. The shadow it cast was almost half my size, but I slipped into it effortlessly, disappearing from view.

Willow gasped, and I grinned. It'd been quite a while since I spent time with someone who was impressed by any of this. My brothers would've just called me out for being too slow.

I slipped back out of the shadow, reappearing before the girl. "That's how it's done."

"Like… this?" Willow walked hesitantly over to the shadow cast by the heavy bag. She stepped onto it carefully then glanced up at me with hope shining in her eyes.

Fighting down a laugh, I said, "I can still see you, wildcat."

Her face fell. "Damn it. What did I do differently than you?"

"Well, for one thing, you just stepped *on* it. To hide in the shadows, you have to slip *into* them."

Willow wrinkled her nose. "I'm trying so hard not to let my brain explode right now."

I couldn't blame her. She'd been in her new body for a few days. I'd had centuries to get used to mine.

"It's all right, we'll try again. Come here." I gestured her forward, and she stepped away from the bag's small shadow. Grasping her shoulders gently, I spun her around to face it again, lowering my head to speak low in her ear. "Think of it like stepping off the edge of a pool into deep water. You don't have to *do* anything. The water is there. Waiting. It wants to envelop you."

Was it my imagination, my untethered longing playing tricks on my mind, or did she soften under my touch? Did her body lean back slightly as if seeking more contact with mine?

"Okay. I'm ready."

"Then step into the shadow. I'll go with you."

We moved forward together, and the shadow welcomed us, drawing us into its depths.

Willow shivered. "Oh, I felt that! Did I do it?"

"You did, little wildcat." I squeezed her shoulders.

I'd helped her along that time, but now that she knew how it worked, I was confident she'd be able to reproduce the effect on her own. I let go of her and stepped back, checking to make sure she stayed hidden in the shadow.

After a moment, she reappeared, breathless with excitement. Her enthusiasm dimmed only slightly when I made her repeat the move over and over until she could slip in and out of the shadow at will.

"Excellent," I said, as she stepped from the shadow once again. "Now let's make it a little more difficult."

"How?"

"I'm going to close my eyes and count to three. While I'm counting, you must find a shadow to hide in. If you can escape the shadow and find a new hiding spot before I catch you, you win. If not, I win."

"Like hide and seek?" She tucked a wisp of dark hair that had escaped her ponytail behind her ear.

"Yes. Exactly like hide and seek. Except if you lose this game in a real fight, a rogue supernatural will kill you and sell your skin to a dark magician," I said dryly.

Willow rolled her eyes, but a flicker of worry passed over her face.

I closed my eyes and counted slowly, listening for her footsteps. I'd promised her I wasn't going to go easy on her, and I had no intention of doing so. The shades certainly wouldn't.

When I reached the end of my count, I glanced over to where her footsteps had stopped. A grin stretched my lips.

Clever minx.

A long bow staff leaned against the wall next to the weapons rack, casting a thin shadow across the wall and floor. With vampire speed, I darted over and pushed her out of the shadow.

Willow reappeared, stumbling backward and landing on her ass.

"Hey!" She looked up at me with wide eyes. "How the hell did you do that?"

"Don't assume you're safe anywhere, wildcat. Not even in the shadows. Next time, move before I find you."

She stood slowly, rubbing her perfectly formed ass. The black pants she wore hugged every curve of her long legs, and I found myself inexplicably jealous of an article of clothing.

I wrenched my gaze away, dropping my eyelids closed. "Again."

We continued like that for several hours. She did well. She was a determined student and a keen observer.

Good. She has so much to learn, and the faster we work, the better.

The more time I spent with this fierce, delicate woman, the harder it became to remember why I needed to keep a barrier up between us.

If I could get these training sessions over with as quickly as possible, I might come out of this with my dignity intact and the shades' corpses at my feet.

18

WILLOW

In.

Out.

Run.

Again. Faster.

In.

Out.

Run.

I slipped from shadow to shadow like a ghost, racing from one to the next so quickly wind whipped the hair back from my face.

My nightly training sessions with Mal were exhilarating and brutal. Every time I thought I'd mastered something, the evil man would throw a new curveball at me, leaving me floundering again.

The first time I'd stepped into a shadow, the first time I'd used my new strength and speed, I'd gotten the most incredible rush. What vampires could do was incredible. It was like being an honest to God superhero.

But Mal was so much better at it all than me. Up against him, I felt like a bumbling idiot who had no idea what she was doing.

Well, the second part is true. I have no fucking idea what I'm doing.

But I was no idiot. And I was determined to hold my own in our next training session, if only to salvage my bruised ego.

In.

Out.

Run.

I sped through the house, challenging myself to slip into smaller and smaller shadows.

Over the past few days, the brothers and I had settled into a strange routine. I spent a lot of my time training with Mal. We were occasionally joined by Jerrett or Sol when they weren't locked in an upstairs library, comparing the markings on the shade's ancient flesh to runes they found in equally ancient tomes.

But every night, we gathered for a meal in a large dining room on the first floor. The food was amazing, although I didn't know where it came from. I never saw any of the men cooking, and I never heard the doorbell ring for delivery.

Regardless of how the food arrived, those dinners had become one of my favorite parts of the day. Something about sitting down around the table transformed the men from stoic hunters to normal, insanely hot guys. They traded banter, fought over the last serving of whatever their favorite dish was, and occasionally regaled me with stories of the strange creatures they'd fought on previous hunts.

Sometimes it was still hard to believe I was the houseguest of three powerful vampires, but in those moments, it didn't really feel like that at all. It felt like being part of a family.

This evening, the brothers had left together to resume their hunt for the shades. I'd offered to go with them, but all three had soundly rejected that idea. So instead, I'd bitten the bullet, sat on the bed in my room upstairs, and made two of the most difficult calls I'd ever had to make.

My phone call with Carly was heartbreaking—the woman had become like a surrogate mother to me, and I was sure she didn't buy my excuse of needing some time off to "work on myself." I had no idea what she guessed was really going on, but worry thickened her voice as she made me promise to call her if I needed anything.

The call with Tony was shorter and less tear-filled, but it'd still hurt. He and I had never been particularly close, and serving drinks at Osiris had been my survival job, not my passion. But quitting felt like putting the final nail in the coffin of my old life, and I'd mourned that loss as I dropped the phone back onto the bed.

I'd hung out in my room for a while, feeling antsy and unsettled, but eventually I couldn't take the waiting any longer. They hadn't given me any explicit instructions to stay out of certain areas of the house, so I'd wandered the halls for a bit, poking my nose into open rooms here and there.

The place was big. Three stories, not including the lower level. Tastefully decorated, with modern, dark wood furniture and high ceilings—the whole place screamed of wealth, but not in an overstated way.

Even though I couldn't hunt with the brothers yet, that didn't mean I couldn't keep training. My current activity had started with a simple attempt to slip into the shadow of an ornate metal sculpture on the first floor. Things had escalated from there, and now I raced from shadow to shadow, whipping around corners and dashing down hallways. I figured there was no harm in it. The brothers would never even know as long as I didn't—

The edge of my shoulder clipped a vase as I darted into what looked like a large study.

It wobbled on the tall tabletop for an agonizing second, then tipped sideways.

My heart lodged in my throat.

Time seemed to slow as I spun on my heel, diving back to catch the vase before it shattered on the floor. I clutched it to my chest like the world's most valuable football, tongue hanging out as I panted in relief.

"*This* is why you don't run in the house, dummy," I muttered. "Everything in here costs more than your entire apartment."

I set the vase back on the table with shaking hands then crept downstairs. These guys didn't seem to be overly materialistic, but I didn't want to risk getting kicked out of their house for destroying their property. As resistant as I'd been to coming here at first, I was starting to realize just how much I needed them.

An hour later, I was in the basement training room doing my best impression of Jackie Chan on the heavy bag when the scent of leather reached my nose. A moment later, a shadow fell across the doorway.

Mal.

I didn't even need to look to know it was him.

"How'd your hunt go?" I asked, grabbing the swinging bag with both hands to still it.

"Not well." He stalked into the room, his dark mood rolling in with him like a storm cloud. "We've lost all trace of the creatures. They've either left the city or they're hiding somewhere out of our reach."

I smoothed back the wisps of hair that had escaped my ponytail, frowning. "I don't understand. Isn't that a good thing?"

He cocked his head at me. "Imagine I'm your enemy. Now, would you rather know where I am or not?"

As he spoke the last words, he moved quickly, slipping into a shadow so fast I lost sight of him. My heart rate picked up, and I glanced uneasily around the room. "Um… I'd rather know."

"Exactly."

Mal's voice came from behind me. I whipped around, my eyes darting back and forth.

"So… you're done hunting for the night?" I asked. If I could keep him talking, maybe I could follow the sound of his voice.

"I didn't say that, wildcat."

The teasing, predatory purr came from behind me again, and I spun. Damn it, how was he moving so fast? I hadn't caught any sign of him.

"Oh yeah? What are you hunting?"

I swiveled my head, my gaze tracking across the room.

Come on. Just a glimpse. A hint of movement.

A second later, I got more than a glimpse. Mal's large form came barreling toward me, slow enough that I could see him this time, but still too fast for me to react in time.

Before I knew what was happening, he'd lifted me off my feet and flipped me onto my back. It was a testament to his strength and control that despite the speed of the movement, I landed gently. He crouched over me, his face hovering above mine.

"You, little wildcat. I'm hunting you."

I swallowed as his dark gaze burned into me. He was on edge tonight, frustrated and restless. Thinking of training with him right now sent a thrill of nervousness and anticipation through me. Mal usually seemed so unflappable, but tonight he definitely looked like he could be... flapped.

I just wasn't sure I was prepared to handle the consequences of that.

"Well, it looks like you caught me." I laughed awkwardly, sitting up and scooting away when he finally leaned back.

"Yes. I did. Far too easily." He looked thoughtful as he crouched on the balls of his feet, elbows resting on his thighs. "We've been focusing on defensive tactics, but it's time you learned some offense."

"You mean like fighting?"

Butterflies exploded in my stomach. I was supposed to fight this man? This tower of ferocious strength and grace?

I wasn't short, but he had at least ten inches of height on me—and about a hundred pounds of muscle. Even with my boosted strength and speed, I had a very strong suspicion I was about to get my ass handed to me.

"I mean exactly like fighting, wildcat."

Mal stood, running both hands through his shaggy dark hair. I couldn't stop my gaze from zeroing in on his biceps—the way they bunched and contracted as he moved, straining against the sleeves of his soft gray long-sleeved tee. His upper arm was the size of my thigh. And I was supposed to fight *that*?

My pride wouldn't let me back down, however. And as he'd pointed out to me about a million times by now, as terrifying as he was, there were creatures out there that were far worse.

Better to face my fear in here, with someone who wouldn't hurt me.

I hope.

As if he could read the thoughts in my head, Mal grinned as

he rolled his sleeves up to his forearms. The feral gleam in his eye made the expression only somewhat comforting.

He extended a large hand down and helped me to my feet.

Then he stepped back, spreading his arms wide. "It's easy, wildcat; I want you to hit me. That's all you have to do. I won't hit back. Just hit me as hard as you can."

I wrinkled my nose. "As *hard* as I can? Are you sure?"

He dipped his head in a nod, his lips quirking. My stomach rolled, but I raised my hands in front of me, curling them into loose fists.

"Oh geez, this feels like a fucking trap," I muttered under my breath.

Mal chuckled darkly. "No trap. As hard as you can."

I bounced lightly on the balls of my feet, taking a few calming breaths through my nose. Then I leapt toward him, using all my vampire speed as I snapped my hand out.

He hadn't lied. He didn't hit back.

But I didn't hit him either.

One second, he was in front of me. The next instant, there was nothing but empty space. He'd moved so fast I'd completely lost sight of him.

I stumbled forward but caught my balance quickly, pivoting on the ball of my foot and launching myself at him again. This time my fist caught the edge of his shoulder as he slipped away.

It was like punching granite, but I resisted the urge to shake out my hand as I swung around to face him. "Ha!"

Mal grinned. "Well done."

"So do I win?"

"No, you just advance to the next round."

Unconsciously, I raised my hands higher. "What round is that?"

"Now I get to try to stop you."

Ah, damn it.

Deciding the element of surprise was probably the only chance I had, I didn't waste time pouting. I launched another attack, my fists flying in a quick volley. He blocked each one easily before spinning me around and pinning my wrist behind my back.

"Try again, wildcat." His breath stirred my hair, and my heartbeat thudded hard in my chest.

We traded blows for several more minutes—and by "traded," I mean, I tried to hit him, and he batted my hands away like they were annoying flies. I did get in a few lucky hits, but nothing that did any real damage. I was beginning to think nothing *could* damage this demi-god of a man.

As we broke apart and circled each other, I noticed his normally steady gaze waver, slipping down. I hesitated, glancing downward myself. My loose-necked t-shirt had slipped off one shoulder as we sparred, revealing the line of my collarbone, the swell of my right breast, and the top of my simple lace bra.

Is he... checking me out?

My skin tingled with awareness, and to test my theory, I shook out my shoulders, readjusting my stance as I let out a breath. The movement worked my t-shirt farther down my arm, showing just a little more of the skin beneath.

Mal's nostrils flared, his rich brown eyes darkening.

Even as his gaze made my skin catch fire, I took his distraction for the gift it was. I launched myself at him, hitting him hard in the side. He let out a grunt, stumbling backward in surprise, and we both went down.

I landed on top of him and sat up, triumph glinting in my eyes. "Do I win now?"

In a flash, Mal rolled us over, wresting back the upper hand. The weight of his large body pressed down on me as his gaze met mine. The humor in his eyes was gone, replaced by the dark wildness I'd seen earlier.

"No, little wildcat." His voice was soft. "You do not win. You cheated."

I struggled to push him off, annoyance rising in me. He couldn't even let me have *one* win? Seriously?

"How is it cheating to use every advantage I can get? You were eyeballing my breasts, and while you were distracted, I hit you. Sounds fucking fair to me!"

"Do you think that move would actually work in a real fight?"

"Maybe!" I pummeled his hard chest with my hands, baring my teeth in frustration.

He grabbed my wrists, pinning them to the floor by my head. His face lowered, so close I could see the small flecks of dark red in his brown irises.

"Do you think creatures made of shadow and desiccated flesh will lust after your body? That they'll be entranced by the sight of your soft skin? No, little wildcat. They won't be distracted so easily."

I twisted under his grip, my breath coming in short gasps as I snarled, "Oh yeah? Then how come it worked on you?"

As if drawn by a magnetic force, his focus drifted downward again. Our struggle on the floor hadn't helped my shirt situation at all. Even more of my bra was showing, and the fabric of the tee had inched up on the bottom as well, revealing a flat strip of my stomach.

Mal sucked in a breath, his muscles going rigid. For a moment that seemed to hang suspended in time, he just stared at that small expanse of naked skin. Then he wrenched his gaze away, looking back up at my face.

A dozen emotions flickered through his eyes, too fast and too intense for me to register most of them.

Lust. Anger. Self-recrimination. Fear.

He shifted slightly, adjusting his grip on my wrists, and my breath caught for a whole new reason.

Mal's body was settled in the cradle of my legs, his muscled weight keeping me pinned to the floor.

And he was rock hard.

19

MALCOLM

THOUGHTS RAN through my head so fast I could barely comprehend them.

My body raged, held in check only by the thinnest thread of self-control. The hunt with my brothers tonight had been frustrating and worrisome, and I'd returned to the house with unspent energy coursing through my veins. The second I walked into this room and saw Willow, tantalizingly disheveled as she worked the heavy bag, I should've walked right back out again.

Nothing good could come of staying. I'd known that.

Yet I hadn't been able to resist—had even convinced myself my motives were entirely selfless. The fact that we'd lost track of the shades meant Willow was in more danger than ever. We had no idea where our enemy lurked, and she needed to know how to defend herself.

I'd stifled the voice in my head that told me I was only doing this because I wanted to touch her smooth skin, to see the wild gleam in her hazel irises as she fought.

Now the wildcat stared up at me, her eyes wide and

unblinking. She'd ceased her struggles, her body softening and giving way under mine. Only her chest moved, her perfect breasts rising and falling with her deep breaths.

She licked her lips, and desire roared through me at the sight of her pink tongue darting out to wet those perfect, bow-shaped lips. I clenched my jaw as my cock pulsed, holding myself stock still to keep from grinding into her.

"Mal..."

Willow's voice was a breathy whisper. The rush of blood in her veins was a siren's call.

"Malcolm," I gritted out. It was the only damned thing I could manage to say.

Her brows furrowed, a little line appearing between them. "What?"

"Malcolm. My name is Malcolm."

"Oh." She blinked up at me, her mouth falling open.

My hands still held her wrists, and the sight of her lying so pliant and vulnerable—so *trusting*—beneath me made me ache to claim her.

To make her mine.

To bury my cock inside her soft warmth and stay there for eternity.

"I'm sorry. I didn't realize. I heard Jerrett call you Mal, and I just assumed..." She trailed off, embarrassment coloring her cheeks. "Jesus. We've never even been properly introduced."

The laugh that burst from my lips should've tamed my arousal, but it only served to heighten it.

This was why Willow was so goddamned alluring. She constantly took me by surprise. We were sprawled across the floor of the training room, locked in a very compromising position as a cloud of lust hovered in the space between us, daring one of us to act.

And this insane woman was worried about being proper.

My laugh settled into a rumbling chuckle, and goose bumps broke out across her skin as her breath picked up again. The warm cherry and almond scent that was uniquely *her* invaded my nostrils, tinged with a combination of arousal and fear.

Smart girl. You should be frightened. Both of us should. Because I'm about to make a very big mistake.

"Wildcat..." My voice was low and thick, and I watched her pupils dilate in response to my words. "When you're looking at me like that, you can call me whatever you want."

Fuck. I can't resist.

My head lowered, my gaze falling to her lips. Willow's hands curled up reflexively, her wrists flexing against my palms as if trying to reach for me.

"Malcolm!" she gasped.

Whether the word was a plea or a warning, the sound of her breathy voice calling my name snapped the last thread of my self-restraint.

Her face rose to meet mine as I dipped my head lower, capturing her perfect mouth in a kiss. She tasted incredible. Sweet and exotic, like some kind of rare fruit—and underneath that, the tangy, coppery taste of the blood coursing through her veins.

I spread her lips with my tongue, her unique, addictive essence overwhelming my senses as she opened to me willingly.

My fangs dropped, and my lips curled back.

Then I froze.

It had been an instinct I couldn't control, but fear lanced

through me as I realized what I'd been about to do. Gasping, I wrenched my head away from hers, rolling off her.

"Goddamnit. I—"

But Willow wasn't done.

Instead of letting go, she clung to me as I rolled, ending up on top of me again. Her warm body pressed against mine, the weight nothing, but the contact between us everything. She plunged her delicate fingers into my hair, tugging lightly at the thick strands as her lips met mine in another searing kiss that dissolved my restraint.

She wants more. How can I deny her?

My wildcat.

The thought thrummed in my mind as I skimmed my hands down the back of her body, palming her ass and pulling her hard against me, easing some of the ache in my balls. She gasped into my mouth, a little moan falling from her lips, and I claimed both sounds with my kiss.

I wanted them all. Every hot breath, every tortured moan.

I wanted to own her pleasure.

Fuck, she already owned mine.

She sat back quickly, grabbing the hem of my shirt and pulling it over my head. She gaped at the sight of my chest and abdomen, and a swell of pride warmed me. My appearance had made plenty of women stop in their tracks over the years, but the way Willow's gaze flickered over my muscles, the way she blushed almost shyly, affected me in a way I hadn't been prepared for.

Her fingertips brushed over my stomach, and a growl tore from my throat.

Wrapping my arms around her, I sat up and pressed her flush against me, grinding my cock into the warmth between her thighs. Only a few pieces of fabric separated us there, and I hated every single one of them.

My tongue delved into her mouth, as if somewhere deep in that kiss was the antidote to this unstoppable craving.

I rolled us again, our bodies still fused together like two halves of a whole. Bracing myself on my forearms, I buried my face in the crook of her neck, losing myself in her sweet scent. She cried out and bucked beneath me when I licked the soft skin, her nails digging into my back as her legs twined around me.

She was wearing too many damned clothes.

But I could fix that.

The fabric of her t-shirt tore like tissue paper as I ripped it down the front, exposing the light blue bra that had captured my attention so completely.

And who could fucking blame me?

The soft lace cupped her perfectly formed breasts, clinging to the sloping curves and revealing just a hint of her dusky pink nipples. They were peaked, hard, begging for attention.

I lowered my head to capture one in my mouth, sucking on it through the fabric of her bra.

"Oh my God..." Willow's eyelids fluttered as she tossed her head restlessly back and forth.

My fangs were still extended, and every sound she made urged on the predator in me. I wanted to sink my teeth into the soft flesh of her breast and lap up the blood that welled. But I couldn't allow myself to go that far. I'd made a vow many years ago, and even though a fog of lust muddled my brain, I knew I wouldn't be able to live with myself if I broke that promise.

And besides, the bond between us was too strong already. If I drank from her, I'd be lost entirely; I couldn't afford to let that happen.

So I satisfied myself with using my sharp incisors to tear at the delicate lace of her bra, shredding it in long gashes as I dragged my teeth over her skin, leaving red marks across her breasts.

My marks.

They would fade quickly as her vampire healing set in, but for the moment, she was mine.

The wildcat was lost to her passion now, as helpless against the pull between us as I was. She'd given up on coherent words and was mumbling curses as she threaded her hands into my hair, trying to bring my mouth even closer to her flushed, tortured breasts. Her body worked against mine, and I could feel her heat and wetness, smell the intoxicating scent of her arousal.

The pattern of thin white scars decorating her body stood out against her flushed skin. I ran my hands down her sides as I traced a path up her neck with my tongue and gazed into her stormy, half-lidded hazel eyes.

I was about to claim another kiss when her expression changed.

Willow's eyes widened at the same time they slipped out of focus, staring past me, unblinking. Her body jerked and went rigid as her breath caught in her throat.

Then she sagged beneath me, her eyelids sliding shut.

20

WILLOW

Malcolm's touch was like a tidal wave, crashing over me and buffeting me about in a turbulent sea of emotions.

It overwhelmed me, consumed me, burned me to ash, and resurrected me.

I'd ever felt anything like it, and my body's response almost terrified me. I'd always liked sex, but I'd never felt such an insatiable, uncontrollable need before. Rational thought died an unceremonious death as a man I barely knew—scratch that, a *vampire* I barely knew—played my body like a finely tuned instrument, and instead of trying to stop him, I urged him on with everything I had.

I ached to feel his hands and lips all over my body and to explore every inch of his in return. It was torture feeling his hard cock grinding against me and not being able to touch it. I wanted to feel the heat of his naked body against mine. I wanted to feel him moving inside me, filling the desperate, indescribable emptiness in my soul I hadn't even known existed until this moment.

I was incomplete, and he could make me whole.

Malcolm's lips were firm and warm, and his sharp teeth sent a shiver of fear and lust through me as they scraped across my sensitized skin. My entire body felt electric, flushed, and almost numb from overstimulation. I couldn't take this. It was too much. Too good.

Speech was impossible. Thought was impossible.

Nothing else existed in the world—only his hands, his mouth, his sharp breaths, and the scent of leather filling my nose.

Then something changed.

Being surrounded by Malcolm had felt almost like an out of body experience, but this was more than that. I truly *was* leaving my body.

As if my soul had suddenly become more dense than my flesh and blood, I felt myself begin to sink. I tried to call out, to grab onto him for support, but it was no use. I felt my body jerk, heard the hitch of my breath.

But the body that lay stiff and frozen beneath Malcolm was no longer mine.

I had no body.

Anchorless and heavy, my soul sank. Through the floor. Through the earth.

Into blackness.

The scrap of consciousness that remained of me screamed in panic and fear—a sound no one could hear.

Was I dreaming? Had I passed out from the intensity of sensations and emotions coursing through me? Or had I dreamed about my interlude with Malcolm too? Maybe none of this was real. Was this some aspect of being a vampire the brothers had forgotten to warn me about? Insane, hot hallucinations interrupted by soul crushing darkness?

I tried to cry out again, but I had no voice here. When I lifted a hand in front of me, I couldn't see it. I wasn't sure if that was because of the pure blackness surrounding me or because my hand just wasn't there anymore.

Then, just as suddenly as it had come, the darkness cleared. I found myself floating under a dim night sky. The shift from sinking to floating made me dizzy, but my stomach didn't lurch—mainly because it wasn't there. I had no form that I could see.

Gray storm clouds hovered threateningly on the horizon, but the weather was calm for now. My attention fell to the sight below me.

An old, abandoned building sat in a clearing. Grass and weeds grew tall around it, and vines had started to creep up one side, crawling through the broken windows. The building was large, with a pointed roof and a large tower on one side near the back. A church, maybe?

Before I could take in more details of the structure, I was distracted by movement in the clearing.

Shades.

I hadn't noticed them at first because their shadowy forms blended so well with the dark, starlit terrain. But there were several of them, drifting fitfully about. Malcolm had told me they'd lost track of the shades they were hunting in New York. Is this where they'd gone? Had there been this many in the city, or had others joined them?

The wind shifted, and the dark clouds rolled in, obscuring the stars. In the waning light, it was impossible to tell if one of the creatures below me was missing a limb. The shades didn't appear to be aware of me floating above them. I tried to move, to drop lower over the crumbling ruin for a better look, but I couldn't.

Whatever force had brought me here was controlling all this, not me.

Then something new caught my eye. A figure walked among the shadow creatures.

I was too far way to see the person clearly. I couldn't tell if it was a man or a woman, though the figure was smaller than the shades surrounding it. A cloak fell over the newcomer's face, obscuring the features beneath. But whoever it was, they looked human—or at least, humanoid.

I strained to move forward; I needed so badly to get closer. The brothers would be so happy if I could give them some new information about this threat. Once they took care of the shades, once they figured out what the creatures wanted with me, maybe I could return to some semblance of a normal life.

But the more I struggled to direct my consciousness, to move toward the ruins, the farther away I seemed to float. Rain began to fall—fat, heavy drops that flew past me, through me. The scent of damp earth rose up to greet me, along with a hint of something else. Something floral and sweet. Jasmine?

The rain picked up, individual drops turning into sheets of water as thunder boomed and lightning lit up the sky. I was drifting away faster now, leaving the shades and the unknown figure behind. But for a brief moment, the newcomer's head lifted toward the sky, and I caught a glimpse of pale white skin.

I wanted to stay, to see more, but there was nothing to hold onto. The ruins and the rain disappeared, and I was left floating in the black abyss again.

Damn it. Whatever I'd just seen had been important. If I'd been able to get closer, maybe I could've picked up some piece of useful information.

My abilities were failing me, just like they had in the training room with Malcolm. I screamed into the darkness again, frustration at being constantly out of my depth bursting out of me.

But the darkness didn't care.

It swallowed up my scream and gave nothing back.

REJOINING my body wasn't gentle or peaceful.

It was like riding a rollercoaster in the dark, unable to see the twists and turns coming but buffeted from all sides, tossed around like a rag doll.

Then my consciousness slammed back into solid flesh, and I woke with a jolt. I sat up, gasping.

I was on the large bed in my new room. For a second, my mind flashed back to the first time I'd woken in this house, and panic flooded my system. But my hands weren't bound now. I wasn't held captive.

My heartbeat slowed slightly with that realization as I blinked. Fog still hovered in my brain, and my body felt heavy and numb. What the hell had just happened? Had any of that been real?

A woman I didn't recognize rushed to my side, fussing over me. "Ah, you're awake! Not too fast, not too fast."

She was older, with a weather-beaten face, silver hair, and bright purple eyes. Despite their odd color, they were warm and kind. But when she pressed on my shoulders, trying to force me back down, my panic resurfaced. Too many strange beings had attacked me in the last week, and my survival instincts kicked into high gear.

"No! Don't touch me!" I slid away from her, scooting toward the other side of the mattress.

A warm hand caught my arm, and my head snapped up. Sol sat on the edge of the bed, his expression serious, his unseeing green eyes trained on my face. He slid his hand down and grasped my fingers gently, stroking his thumb over the back of my hand.

"Sol!" I gasped. My brain was scrambled mush, and his name seemed to be the only word I remembered. "Sol. I... Sol!"

"Shh, it's all right. You have nothing to fear. You're safe. We'll always keep you safe."

He pulled me into his arms, and I clung to him like a child, allowing his strength and stability to envelop me. He smelled amazing, warm and spicy, and the slow cadence of his heartbeat soothed my own.

As I regained my composure, my gaze slid over his shoulder to the older woman. She'd crossed around to this side of the bed and now stood behind him with her arms folded.

"Well, I didn't mean to scare you," she huffed. A Russian accent tinged her words, and she sounded slightly offended.

I pulled away from Sol. "No, you didn't. I was just startled. Who... are you?"

"Willow, this lovely woman is Yuliya. She cooks for us, looks after our house, and keeps my brothers and me in line, don't you, Yuliya?"

Sol's voice was warm as he tipped his head over his shoulder toward her. Yuliya couldn't hide her smile when he spoke. She clearly adored him, and I could see why. Even knowing what he was, even having seen him fight, there was something about Sol that made me feel completely protected. When he promised he would keep me safe, I believed him.

The woman laughed, her purple eyes twinkling. "Somebody must do it, eh? The three of you are barely home—and when you are, you make such a mess! Always broken furniture, holes in walls... dirty dishes."

She poked Sol in the back when she said that last bit, making me suspect he was the worst offender in that area.

Huh. This gorgeous, supernaturally powerful man didn't like doing dishes. I could definitely relate to that, but something about it still struck me as odd. The image of him padding through the kitchen and slipping an empty bowl into the sink was just so... so *human.*

As if he could read my thoughts, he chuckled. "I'm not a slob, I promise. Besides, we can't all use magic to cook and clean like you can, Yuliya."

Magic?

My brain balked at that word, so I let it float on by. I'd already seen more proof than I needed that the supernatural existed, so why not magic too? But I'd deal with processing that information later.

Yuliya poked him again. "True. True! Which is why you're so lucky to have me."

Sol chuckled. "Yuliya was away this past week visiting her coven in Russia. Now that she's back, don't hesitate to ask her if you need anything."

"Yes! Anything you need. Clothes, food, something cleaned, something fixed—I do it all. Goodness, I've replaced all the furniture in this house by now. Twice!" She tsked through her teeth. "Boys. They break so many things."

I was beginning to like the old woman. Something about her presence felt grounding, as if she made all of this more real somehow. She was so solid and down-to-earth, and the way she treated Sol made him seem less like a terrifying creature of the night and more like a regular, if extremely rich, guy. She certainly wasn't afraid of him.

And Sol seemed genuinely attached to her. I trusted him as a judge of character. If he liked her, she must be a good person.

There was a knock on the bedroom door seconds before it opened. Malcolm strode into the room, followed closely by Jerrett. Their attention landed on me immediately, and they both pulled up short. Worried blue and brown gazes raked over my body, as if searching for injuries.

They'd been worried about me.

The realization cracked open a door in my heart, letting light fill the long-empty space.

"Willow." Malcolm's voice was low and rough.

Oh Jesus.

Heat rose in my face as memories flooded me, and I was positive my cheeks were flame red. What had happened between us hadn't been a dream or a hallucination. As much as I might wish otherwise now, it'd been incredibly real. His searing kisses had seemed to steal a part of my soul, and his hands had been warm, calloused, and possessive.

His breath. His teeth on my skin, tearing through my bra and—

Embarrassment opened up a hole in my stomach, and I glanced down at myself. I wore a soft, long-sleeved shirt and stretchy gray pants.

They'd changed my clothes. Again.

That thought alone wasn't nearly as humiliating as what they had changed me *out* of. Had Sol and Jerrett come downstairs and found me like that? Sprawled on the floor, my hair a mess, my shirt ripped open, and my bra shredded? Sol wouldn't have been able to see me, but I had no doubt his other senses would've told him exactly what Malcolm and I had been doing. And that idea was somehow worse.

How did I let that happen?

One minute we'd been fighting, and the next, I'd been completely consumed by a man whose real name I didn't even know.

I peeked up through my eyelashes. All three brothers were still watching me. Even with my focus glued to the bedspread in front of me, I could feel the weight of their gazes. Yuliya's too.

"I think I had a vision," I blurted.

What I'd seen in my dream felt important, but more than that, I needed to interrupt my current train of thought. If I lingered too long on what I'd done with Malcolm, of what his brothers might know, I'd devolve into a full-blown freak out.

Thank God, the vision had pulled me away. If it hadn't, I was sure Malcolm and I would've...

Shoving away a fresh new wave of images and feelings, I forced myself to look up. "I saw something."

"A vision?" Sol tilted his head.

I nodded, twisting a lock of hair around my fingers. "Yes. One minute I was... in my body. And then I sort of *fell* out of myself. I sank through the earth and floated in a black void. I couldn't speak or smell or see. I was nothing."

"Shit," Jerrett murmured.

Sol shushed him and turned to me. "A black void. Go on."

The intensity of his sightless stare made my skin prickle. If I'd thought the brothers might not believe me, that they'd laugh and call me crazy, I should've known better.

I was part of their world now. And things like this were real in their world.

Taking a deep breath, I continued.

"Then the blackness faded. I hovered in the sky. I don't know if I was flying or floating, but none of it felt like it was under my control. I was just... there. I could see things below me, but I was too far away to make out everything."

"What did you see?" Jerrett pushed his black hair out of his eyes.

Sol gave my hand a squeeze. It felt good to have his fingers interlinked with mine. Comforting. Strengthening.

"I saw an old building in a clearing. An abandoned church, I think. It was night, and there were—"

I broke off, suddenly afraid to speak it out loud. As if what I'd seen wasn't a vision of what was but a premonition of what could be, and giving voice to it would make it real.

"There were what?"

A muscle in Malcolm's jaw ticked. His expression was hard, but I couldn't identify the emotion behind it.

"There were shades. Several of them. Six, maybe seven? I didn't get an exact count; it was almost impossible to tell them from the surrounding shadows sometimes. They were in front of the church. I wanted to get closer, but I couldn't do it."

"You were stuck?" Sol asked.

"Yes! It was like I was suspended in space. I couldn't move at all; there was nothing to grab onto. When I fought harder, I felt myself being pulled away, and I couldn't fight against that either. The darkness sucked me back in."

I paused, gathering my thoughts, trying to remember everything I'd seen. A pale face flashed in my mind.

"And there was someone with them. Someone who wasn't one of them. The shades were all gathered around this person, but they didn't attack it—like it was someone important." I shook my head, letting out a sigh. "I'm sorry. I tried to see more, but I couldn't."

The brothers were quiet for a moment. Yuliya's sharp purple eyes darted from the three of them to me and back again. I shifted on the bed, uncomfortable with all the attention. I'd never had anyone listen to me so intently.

For as long as I could remember, I'd had strange, vivid dreams. I'd tried describing them to Kyle on occasion but gave up after watching his eyes glaze over from boredom one too many times.

This was more than just a dream. Whatever the vision had been, it meant something. It was important. Of course, these men would be interested in it. Still, it was strange to feel so… *heard.*

Picking at a loose thread in the comforter, I sighed. "I don't know what it means. I don't know where the church is or how I saw all that. But it felt real."

"It was real. You have the Sight." Sol's voice was quiet, almost reverent. "An old gift. Most vampires don't have it anymore. It's more common in other supernaturals, but even then, it's an incredibly rare thing."

"So what does it mean? Why did I have this vision?"

"You're connected to the shades somehow. Your spirit went searching for them." Malcolm broke away from Jerrett to pace across the room, his back to us.

Was it my imagination, or was he avoiding *my* gaze now? Shit. Did he regret what had happened between us? Despite my own misgivings and embarrassment, that thought stabbed like a hot knife.

Jesus. I spent nine years feeling nothing, and now I feel too much. I can't stop *feeling.*

I ripped my attention away from Malcolm's tense shoulders

and looked back at Sol. "Connected? How? What does that mean?"

Sol squeezed my hand one more time then let go, rising to his feet.

"Something is drawing your Sight to them. If you can learn to control your power, you won't be helpless in your visions. You'll be able to move your consciousness, to have agency. You won't be able to interact with the things in your visions, no seer can do that. But if you can identify the shades' location, that's enough. You can help us track them."

"And then what?"

His strange green eyes blazed. "Then we'll hunt them down and kill them."

21

WILLOW

I LAY in bed and stared up at the ceiling, listening to the slow *thud... thud... thud* of my heartbeat. As strange as it was to be a vampire with a pulse, I was grateful this particular part of vampiric myth had been wrong. I'd rather have a heartbeat than not, even if the rhythm was much slower than it'd been when I was human.

After peppering me with a few more questions about the nature of my vision, Sol had told me to get some rest and assured me we'd talk more in the evening. I'd almost laughed at his words.

Get some rest? Yeah, sure thing. No problem.

My mind raced in circles at a thousand miles a minute. I was exhausted and wired at the same time, but sleep refused to come. It was probably around one or two in the afternoon, though the dark room gave no indication of that. I felt jet lagged, like my brain and body couldn't agree on what time it was.

More of those visions will come. And I have to learn to control them. How the hell do I do that?

Sol had seemed awed by the revelation of my strange new ability, and Malcolm had seemed almost angry—though I wasn't sure if he was mad about the Sight or something else. Jerrett's perma-smirk made it a little hard to tell what he thought of all this, but he definitely believed in the vision I'd had.

Would the brothers let me join them on their hunt if I could pinpoint the shades' location?

Did I want that?

Yes.

The simple truth of my answer caught me off guard. But I did want it. The shades were more than just a threat to me. If the brothers were right, they were a threat to humans and possibly even other supernaturals. If I could save some other poor woman from the fate that had befallen me, shouldn't I do it?

The dream I'd held onto for so many years—the bakery with a blue door and the pristine white counters, filled with the smell of lemon and vanilla—had died the night I almost did. But a new dream had slowly been coalescing to take its place.

A dream of a purpose. Of a place in the world.

Sol, Jerrett, and Malcolm were hunters. Their self-appointed duty was to keep others safe.

What better purpose was there than that?

As unnerving as the events and discoveries of the past week had been, I was starting to realize maybe I *didn't* want to get off this crazy ride.

And that scared the shit out of me.

I sighed and slipped out of bed, running my fingers through my dark hair. There was no point trying to sleep; I was just stewing in my own confused thoughts. I needed a distraction.

As if responding to my silent request, my stomach let out a low growl.

I bit back a chuckle as I patted my belly. *Good point, buddy. Food is always an* excellent *distraction.*

I stepped out into the long hallway. My eyes were definitely sharper now than they had been, because I could make out the hardwood floors and smooth, cream-colored walls despite the almost pitch blackness of my surroundings. A grandfather clock along the wall told me it was just after 2 p.m.

It was almost impossible to believe the world outside was bright with sunlight right now.

That was one thing I missed. Light. *Real* light, and the warmth of the sun shining down on my skin. This house was beautiful, but it was dark and cold. Maybe the brothers didn't notice because they'd been here so long, but I certainly did.

Keeping my footsteps light, I tiptoed down the stairs, caressing the rich mahogany banister as I made my way down. Jesus, these guys were *not* in need of money. Were all vampires this rich? It wouldn't surprise me. If immortal beings invested wisely for several hundred years, they could accrue a fortune.

I hadn't visited the kitchen during my shadow running excursion, but I found it after a few minutes of searching and flipped on the warm under-cabinet lights.

My jaw dropped.

It looked like something out of my wet dreams—high ceilings, dark wood cabinets, pristine marble counters, and a large breakfast bar with high stools. The fridge itself was bigger than the front door of my apartment.

When I opened it, my gaze landed first on a large stack of blood bags.

I grabbed one, ripped it open, and downed the contents in less than a minute. Then I opened another and drank it more slowly, savoring it a little. There was still something flat about bagged blood, something bland and cold, but it satisfied the burning hunger inside me.

For a moment, I imagined what fresh blood would taste like. *Rich and warm, I bet. Smooth and full of layered flavors.*

Unbidden, my stomach grumbled again, despite the fact that I'd just eaten.

I shivered. As delicious as that sounded, the idea of what I'd have to *do* to get fresh blood made me slightly queasy.

I closed the fridge and tossed the empty bags into the trash.

Now that the pang of blood-hunger had eased, a new kind of hunger took its place—one I was much more familiar with. I hadn't baked in what felt like forever, and this kitchen was too amazing not to put to good use. The beautiful oven was so pristine I was sure it'd never been touched. It was a sin to have a piece of equipment like that and not use it.

If I lived here, really lived here, this kitchen would smell like vanilla and chocolate every day.

The brothers didn't exactly seem like the baking types, but Yuliya must be, because the kitchen was amazingly well stocked. Eggs, butter, and milk sat in the fridge next to the blood bags. And in the corner of the kitchen, a large door led to a walk-in pantry.

Gleaming cupcake trays, cake tins, spatulas, and whisks lined one shelf. I found flour and sugar right away, along with a wide variety of chocolates, vanilla pods, and exotic spreads.

I scooped up everything I needed and brought it back into the kitchen with me. Then I rolled up my sleeves and threw my hair into a messy bun, already feeling calmer. Sifting, measuring, and stirring were almost meditative for me, and as the batter came together, my brain finally stopped whirling.

I was just putting the second batch of cupcakes in the oven

when a noise behind me made me jump. I slammed the oven door and whipped around guiltily, as though I'd been caught stealing instead of baking.

"I'm sorry! I couldn't sleep!" I blurted.

Jerrett sauntered into the kitchen, and my jaw nearly dropped. He wore only a pair of deep blue pajama pants, slung low across his hips. His waist was strong and lean, and the grooves of his abs looked incredible in the warm golden light. His shoulders were broad, his arms muscled and corded. He was taller than Sol, but a bit shorter than Malcolm, and unlike Malcolm's huge, dominating frame, Jerrett's body was leaner, sharper. He had tattoos on each side of his neck, one on his bicep, and one on his chest.

Forget rock star. He looks like a fucking rock god.

My thoughts must've been visible on my face, because his ice-blue eyes heated and a cocky smirk broke out on his face.

"That's okay. I couldn't either."

"Couldn't what?" I asked lamely, blinking several times—as if that would somehow make this man less blindingly attractive.

His smirk widened. "Sleep."

"Oh, right! Me neither."

He chuckled, sweeping a hand through his shock of dark hair. "Yeah, I think we've established that."

"Oh. Right." I closed my eyes. *Come* on, *Willow. Be cool.*

"So what are you doing?" Jerrett walked farther into the kitchen, peering around at the ingredients and utensils spread around the counters.

"Sorry." I suddenly felt incredibly presumptuous for sneaking down to their kitchen in the middle of the day and rooting through the pantry without even asking. "I… I bake when I get anxious. I'll do the dishes in a sec, don't worry. And I'll pay for all the ingredients."

Jerrett shot me a look like I was crazy. "No, you won't. You're our guest. Besides, it's not like we were using this stuff."

I grinned, the nerves in my stomach unclenching. "I figured none of you guys were big into baking."

"Nah. But damn, maybe we should've been." He gazed down at the chocolate cupcakes cooling on a wire rack. "These smell fucking incredible."

Pride inflated my chest like a balloon. "You can try one, if you want. Let me frost it first though."

Jerrett looked on with interest while I mixed up a buttercream frosting with orange peel in it. It was incredibly hard to focus with him hovering behind me. I could feel the warmth radiating from his skin, and his smoky scent mingled with the smell of the cupcakes, making my mouth water.

I dipped a finger in the frosting to taste it, wanting to make sure I got the ratio of sweet to citrus right. When I brought it to my mouth, a low, deep hum came from behind me. The sound sent little shocks of lightning ricocheting through my body, and heat pooled in my belly.

"I want a taste."

Jerrett's voice was teasing and commanding at the same time. A flush crept up my cheeks as I looked up and found him watching me expectantly. I dipped my finger into the frosting again, and Jerrett reached out, taking my hand and bringing it to his mouth.

His lips closed around my finger.

Except, it wasn't my finger.

It couldn't be.

There was no way I had this many nerve endings in the tip of my finger. His warm, wet mouth might as well be clamped around my nipple. Or my clit.

My jaw fell open, a sharp, shocked breath escaping as he worked his tongue around my fingertip, licking off every bit of frosting.

I couldn't tear my focus away from his sharp blue eyes, and he didn't seem to want to let me. He gazed at me with an almost unnerving intensity as he slowly slid my finger out of his mouth.

Reclaiming my hand and trying to put the discombobulated pieces of myself back together, I stammered, "Um, Jerrett, I… Malcolm and I, we—"

Crap. I really didn't want to tell him about what Malcolm and I had done on the floor of the training room. But I had to, before he got the wrong idea.

Jerrett's smile returned, the ring in his lower lip glinting in the light.

"Don't worry about it, Will. I know Mal has a thing for you. It's pretty fucking obvious. Sol does too." He tugged his lip ring into his mouth, his grin positively wicked. "Good thing I don't mind sharing."

22

WILLOW

I BLINKED, my brows furrowing.

Then the full meaning of his words sank in.

Heat tore through my body like an inferno at the same time nervous embarrassment flooded my cheeks.

"I... we... I..."

I would've kept repeating those two words over and over like a broken record if Jerrett hadn't stroked a knuckle down my cheek.

"Relax, Will. Just putting it out there. You already shared us once, the night we turned you. And it was incredible. This could be even better than that."

My body unconsciously leaned into his touch. His words had left me so turned on I was a heartbeat away from climbing him like a tree and rubbing myself all over his naked torso, just to ease some of the desperate ache inside me.

What was it with these men? How did they manage to break down every defense, every barrier I had?

Because as crazy as the idea was, I was seriously considering taking him up on his offer.

But that's not me.

Is it?

Jerrett must've read my expression again and seen the imminent existential breakdown as I grappled with this new, wilder side of myself. He tapped me gently under the chin before turning me back around to face the bowl of frosting I'd completely forgotten about.

"Back to working your magic, sweetheart. I'm still hungry."

I gratefully took the escape he offered me, digging a butter knife into the frosting and slathering it on a cupcake with shaking hands. The brothers didn't have any pastry piping equipment, but the simple act of spreading frosting into whorls and peaks calmed my frayed nerves. My hand was steadier when I turned back to Jerrett and offered it to him.

He brushed his hair out of his eyes then took it, peeling the wrapper down on one side.

I watched him anxiously, chewing on my lower lip. Kyle had always been really critical of my baking. He'd claimed his harsh critiques were all in the name of helping me improve, but after a while, I'd stopped offering him any of my creations because I didn't want to be torn down every time I did. Since then, plenty of strangers had told me they loved my desserts, but worry still churned in my stomach as Jerrett took his first bite.

His mouth closed, but he didn't chew. His eyes widened.

Worry turned to panic, and I ran through the recipe in my head. Had I left out some critical ingredient by mistake?

"I'm sorry. You don't have to finish it if it isn't good. Maybe I—"

"Holy shit! Fuck me! This is un-fucking-believable."

His words were muffled by the food in his mouth, but the awe in his voice was unmistakable. He took another big bite, his blue eyes gleaming. A tiny bit of frosting hung on his upper lip, and I was struck by the sudden urge to lick it off.

I watched him devour the whole cupcake. It was probably incredibly rude to stare at someone while they ate, but I couldn't tear my eyes away from the sight of him enjoying my creation.

I'd made that look appear on his face.

When he finished, he set the empty wrapper on the counter and looked up at me, the lock of black hair falling over his eyes again. "Well, that settles it. You can't ever leave us now. Fucking good goddamn, Will, that was one of the best things I've ever eaten!"

I blushed, more thrilled by his exuberant compliment than I should've allowed myself to be.

"Well, I don't have plans to leave anytime soon. At least not until we figure out what those shades are after and how to stop them."

Jerrett's expression darkened. He crossed the kitchen and sank onto a stool at the bar. "Yeah. About that. According to a werewolf friend of ours, there've been shade attacks in other cities on the east coast over the past several weeks. He didn't have a ton of details, but this guy is well connected in the supernatural community. He'd know."

My brow furrowed. I spread frosting on two more cupcakes, then brought them over to the bar with me, settling onto a stool next to Jerrett and offering him one. "You think those attacks are related to the one on me?"

"I'd bet anything they are. Shades aren't all that common."

I took a small bite of my own cupcake, trying not to notice the way Jerrett's piercing blue eyes tracked every movement of my lips. Hell, I'd ogled him while he ate, so I could hardly complain if he did the same to me. It did make keeping my mind on the current conversation a bit difficult though.

Clearing my throat, I forced my thoughts back to the problem at hand. "Have the shades been attacking humans?"

"Both. A mix of humans and supernaturals. He said at least one victim had runes carved into them like you, but I don't know if they all did."

A chill worked its way down my spine. Jesus. That was horrific.

"What exactly are these things?" I asked.

Jerrett pushed his hair out of his eyes. "That's the problem. We don't really know. The word 'shade' is pretty much a blanket term for any resurrected creature that can take physical form. They're undead. But what these shades *were* when they were alive? That, we don't know."

"But that's an important piece of the puzzle?"

"Yeah, probably. Once we know what they were, we'll have a better idea how to fight them. And maybe it'll help us figure out what they're after too. Then we'll just need you to tell us where they are."

My stomach flipped. *Right. No pressure.*

Jerrett leaned back, starting in on his second cupcake. After a few bites, he held the half-eaten confection out in front of him, looking at it almost wonderingly. "Good. Fucking. Lord. That might be the *best* thing I've ever eaten."

"Better than blood?" I asked teasingly.

He raised a pierced brow, his expression wicked in the dim light. "Depends whose blood it is, sweetheart."

Warmth flooded my veins again. I was starting to feel like a hormonal teenager with a crush… or three.

To distract him, and myself, I blurted, "Can I ask you a question?"

He set the cupcake down and crossed his arms over his muscled chest. "Sure, Will. Shoot."

"Why do you guys only drink from blood bags? I mean, I'm sure they're better than nothing, but... well, you know. They're..."

"They're not the same," he finished for me.

"No. I mean, I've never had fresh blood. But even I can tell it's not the same. Why is that all you drink? It's not like you'd have to kill someone to drink their blood, right?" A flush crept up my cheeks. "According to Google, some people might be pretty into that. They said it feels really good."

Jerrett nodded. He took his time answering me, his gaze never leaving my face.

"You're not wrong. Most vampires prefer fresh human blood. You'll know by now that the bagged shit is just that. Shit. But it's good enough. It keeps us going, right?"

I ducked my head thoughtfully. "Yeah, it does."

"And we can still enjoy human food. Even if it doesn't quite satisfy the body, it satisfies the mind. Don't ever underestimate the importance of that." His eyes lit suddenly. "Hey, can you make tiramisu sometime? I haven't had that in fucking forever."

"Sure. You probably have all the ingredients on hand. Yuliya keeps your pantry insanely well-stocked."

Jerrett grinned. "She did that for you, sweetheart. Sol told her you like to bake, and she might've gone a little overboard conjuring things."

A laugh burst from me. "Holy shit! I guess that makes more sense than you guys owning cupcake tins." Then I swallowed. "Jerrett? You didn't answer my question."

"Hmm?"

"Why don't you drink fresh blood?"

"Because of Mal."

His jaw snapped shut the moment the words were out of his mouth, like he wished he hadn't spoken.

I bit my lip. "*Malcolm* doesn't want you drinking blood? Why?"

Jerrett eased out a breath, dipping his finger into the frosting on his cupcake and licking it off.

"That's his story to tell, Will, not mine. I hope he does tell you someday. It'll help you understand why he is the way he is."

"You mean grouchy all the time?"

"Ha! Some might call it stoic, but yeah. Grouchy works too. He's not mad at you, Will. Ever. When he gets like that, it's because he's mad at himself."

"Mad at himself for what?"

Jerrett rubbed the back of his neck, his palm covering the tattoo that ran along one side. "He made a mistake a long time ago that I don't think he'll ever forgive himself for. He'll probably spend the rest of his life trying to atone for it."

Pity and unease twisted my stomach into a knot. The rest of his life? That could be hundreds, *thousands* of years. What could he possibly have done that would require that much penance?

I opened my mouth to ask another question, but Jerrett shook his head. "I can't tell you more, Will. Mal is my brother, and I respect the fuck out of him. He's too hard on himself, and I wish he could see that. But I'm not gonna go around spilling his secrets."

My jaw eased shut. The teasing gleam still flickered in Jerrett's blue eyes, but his expression was serious. The way he stood by his brother so adamantly made warmth bloom in my chest—both for the man in front of me and for Mal.

"I understand." I leaned back, nodding. "Thanks for talking, Jerrett. It means a lot."

His playful demeanor returned, and he scooped the remaining half-cupcake off the bar. "Sweetheart, anytime. And you throw in delicious shit like this on top of the pleasure of your company? Well, you're never gonna get rid of me now."

A ripple of pleasure washed over me. He said the words as lightly and easily as anything, but he couldn't know how much they meant to me. It'd been so long since I'd been flirted with, appreciated, or wanted. It made me feel special—maybe not to the whole world, but to a blue-eyed vampire rock star with a wicked tongue and a big heart.

And that was enough for me.

I grinned. "That's okay. I'm not in any hurry to get rid of—"

The sound of footsteps on the stairs reached my ears, and I broke off, cocking my head. Jerrett heard it too and was on his feet before Sol and Malcolm burst into the room.

"What is it?"

Jerrett's voice was sharp, the hunter in him rising to the surface.

Sol inhaled deeply, and I blushed at the hunger that swept over his face at the scent of my cupcakes. I kind of wanted to sit around feeding these guys for days, just watching the expressions on their faces while they ate my creations.

Then again, maybe there was a better way to put that sexy, hungry look on his face.

"Thomas just called," Malcolm answered, ripping me from my thoughts. "There's a problem in the subway lines. Goblins have been getting out of control, attacking commuters and disrupting trains."

23

WILLOW

"Ah, fuck." Jerrett grimaced. "Give me two minutes."

He darted from the room, and I looked between Malcolm and Sol. The dark, broad-shouldered vampire was still refusing to meet my gaze, so I focused on his brother.

"What does that mean? Why did this Thomas guy call you?"

"Thomas is a werewolf friend of ours. He trades in information and has his ear to the ground in most supernatural circles. He helps us keep an eye out for unusual activity," Sol answered.

The timer on the oven beeped, and I jumped. I'd completely forgotten about my second batch of cupcakes. I grabbed the oven mitt off the counter and pulled the tin out, setting it on the wire rack before turning back to the men.

"And this—the goblins attacking—is unusual?"

Malcolm nodded, looking agitated. "Yes. Goblins are about the most harmless creatures that exist in our world. If they're attacking people, something is very wrong."

"Could this have something to do with the shades? Are they back?"

Sol's lips quirked up on one side. "There's only one way to find out."

I realized then that he and Malcolm were both dressed in tactical wear—the dark, breathable clothes they wore when they went out on a hunt. Jerrett must've run upstairs to get ready too.

I licked my lips. "I want to come with you."

Malcolm's brows shot up. "*What*? No. Absolutely—"

"Get dressed."

Sol's voice cut through Malcolm's deep rumble like a hot knife through butter, and I hesitated. I'd never heard Sol disagree with Malcolm before. Though they were obviously a team, Malcolm was also clearly the leader.

"Hurry. We need to leave soon," Sol added.

I broke out of my stasis and rushed from the kitchen, leaving the two headstrong brothers to work out their differences of opinion without me. Somehow, I felt confident Sol would win this one.

In my bedroom, I threw on a dark t-shirt and stretchy, skin-hugging pants that let me move easily. I pulled my hair into a rough ponytail as I galloped back down the stairs.

The three men waited in the kitchen, and as I'd suspected, Sol had been the one to get his way. Malcolm didn't look pleased at all, but he didn't object further. Instead, he turned and led us into what turned out to be a large attached garage. Several gleaming cars were parked in an orderly row.

We all piled into a dark silver BMW, with Malcolm behind the wheel.

It was only when the garage door rose, and the car began to back out of the garage that an obvious thought struck me.

“Wait!” I was in the back with Sol, but I practically dived for the steering wheel. “The sun! Don’t—”

“It’s all right, Willow tree.” Sol caught me, settling me back into my seat. “There’s a protection charm on the windows that absorbs the sun’s rays. It’s not an easy enchantment to come by, but we keep one of our cars spelled at all times in case of emergencies. We’ll be fine.”

Just a few hours ago, I’d been thinking of how much I missed sunshine, but now my heart hammered against my ribs as Malcolm pulled out of the driveway.

But my skin didn’t catch fire or even let off a puff of smoke.

I didn’t feel the terribly agony of being burned alive.

In fact, the interior of the car stayed dim, as if it were twilight inside this small metal box. Outside, I could see the world lit with sunshine, but none of it reached us.

“Holy shit.” I peered out the window as we sped down the road.

Sol chuckled. “Glad you like it.”

It took us almost thirty minutes to reach our destination. Apparently, traffic in Manhattan moved just as slow for vampires as it did for everyone else.

Malcolm pulled over under the shadow of a tall building on 96th Street. A large man with the hairiest forearms I’d ever seen loitered under the scaffolding set up in front of the building. When he saw us, he lifted his chin and walked over.

The brothers slid out of the car. Sol extended a hand back to me as Malcolm conferred briefly with the new man—Thomas, I was guessing. A trickle of fear crawled down my spine as I stepped out onto the shadowy street. I was out of direct sunlight, but it still felt terrifying to be exposed like this. The air felt uncomfortably warm, and I had to assume that was due to ambient light from the sun.

Malcolm handed his keys to Thomas, clapped him on the shoulder, then led us down the sidewalk a short distance.

We passed over a subway grate, and Sol squeezed my hand. "Here."

Before I could ask what he meant, Jerrett and Malcolm disappeared into the shadows below the grate.

My jaw dropped. "How did they...?"

"It's just like shadow walking. Let the shadows pull you in."

When he finished speaking, Sol too dissolved into the darkness of the tunnel below me. I clenched my jaw, my stomach roiling with nerves.

Oh geez. Well, you were the one who asked to join them, Willow. Don't make Sol look bad for vouching for you.

Not giving myself any more time to dwell on the absolute weirdness of this, I took a small step forward, allowing the shadows below my feet to pull me in. I slipped through the grate as if it didn't even exist, and a moment later, I found myself standing in the dark tunnel of the B train.

We set off through the darkness, the noise of trains rumbling in the distance mixing with my heartbeat in my ears. When a train sped toward us on the tracks, its yellow headlights gleaming in the darkness, I almost peed my badass vampire pants. But Jerrett pulled me against the wall, and we sank into the shadows while the train roared past.

After several more minutes of walking in silence, we reached a new tunnel that intersected ours. Malcolm veered into it. There were no tracks on the ground, and the walls were rough and uneven, as if they'd been carved out by crude instruments.

"What is this place?" I whispered.

"Goblin tunnel." Sol's voice came from beside me, and his hand still gripped mine. The darkness was thicker here, almost impenetrable.

"They made this?"

"Yeah." Jerrett's voice floated back from up ahead. "They create offshoots from the main subway lines and live off rats and scraps. There's enough junk tossed out down here to support a pretty big colony of goblins. Shit, if the health department knew, they'd probably give them an award for helping keep New York clean."

I chuckled at that. "So they're like underground pigeons?"

"*Rats* are underground pigeons," Sol corrected. "Goblins are more like—" He broke off suddenly, sniffing the air. "Damn it. I smell shades. They were here."

"Shit. Come on!"

Jerrett darted forward, and we followed, speeding through the tunnel as it twisted and turned beneath the streets of Manhattan.

A few moments later, I could smell it too—the fetid scent of decay that always seemed to cling to the shades. Low, keening cries met my ears, chilling my blood. Lights came into view up ahead, and we slowed our steps.

Dozens of small torches gave off a strange blue glow, illuminating a sea of round, stubby faces with gray-brown skin.

Goblins.

They stood about three feet tall, dressed in a mishmash of rags and garbage. Their blunt teeth were bared in snarls, and it looked like the ones in the front with torches were protecting others that filled the tunnel behind them.

Malcolm held up his hands in a non-threatening gesture, though it was hard for someone as big and powerful as him to look anything but threatening.

"We mean you no harm."

One of the goblins in front let out a stream of guttural sounds, shaking the torch clutched in his fist.

I furrowed my brows. "What?"

The leader repeated the sounds, his voice rising in pitch. Behind him, the wailing intensified. I peered through the crowd of goblins around him to the ones in the back. Several bodies lay unnaturally still on the ground. Dead? Or injured?

"They were attacked," I whispered. "Look."

Malcolm started to step forward, but the goblins pressed closer together, muttering words I couldn't understand as they raised their torches threateningly. It reminded me a little of the scene in *Return of the Jedi* where the ewoks threaten Leia, and I would've smiled if the scene weren't so heartbreaking. There was nothing the goblins could do to stop Malcolm if he chose to continue forward. Their threats were meaningless against a creature of his strength.

Just like they'd probably been against the shades.

But Malcolm stopped, holding out his hands placatingly. He spoke in a low voice, his words meant for us. "So this is why goblins have been wreaking havoc on the subway lines. The shades attacked their colony."

"Are the shadow creatures still here?"

"No," Sol answered me. "Their scent is strong, but not fresh. They've been gone for several hours, at least."

I stared at the round, rough-featured faces before us, feeling helpless. What could we do? The shades were long gone, and it was too late to protect the goblins from their attack. They didn't seem to want our help with their injured or dead either.

Sol's hand was a reassuring anchor, and I squeezed it tighter.

Then I jumped as cold, rough fingers grabbed my other hand. Breathing hard, I looked down.

A small goblin, a female maybe, tugged on my hand again. She had no torch, and her face appeared shadowed and gaunt. She spoke several guttural words then pressed a crumpled up piece of paper into my palm. Frowning, I raised it toward the light, smoothing it out as best as I could.

It was part of an ad torn from a magazine. A family sat on a couch together watching TV. Two children were curled up in between their parents, who gazed down at them adoringly.

The goblin grunted, pointing emphatically to the middle of the picture.

Understanding dawned, and my blood chilled.

"Their kids." I swallowed. "The shades didn't just attack them. I think the monsters stole their kids."

"Do you scent anything, Sol?"

Malcolm's tone was dark, as if he knew what the answer was going to be before he heard it. He probably did. Hell, *I* did.

"No. Nothing. I've lost the trail."

Malcolm cursed under his breath. "Damn it. How did they slip away from us again? If they truly have the goblin children, we should be able to scent *them* at least."

"We should. They must've used some kind of masking spell or something to block the scent."

"Fuck a fucking duck." Jerrett kicked at a metal beam along one wall. The metal dented, and he winced slightly.

We'd spent the past several hours roaming the subway tunnels under Manhattan. After the first hour, slipping into the shadows while trains rattled past had become second nature to me.

But we had nothing to show for our efforts.

We'd followed the shades' scent for a while, losing it occasionally before picking it up again. And then suddenly, it had just vanished.

The trail was dead, and we all knew it. But Sol and Jerrett continued to poke around ahead of us, slipping down offshoot tunnels briefly before rejoining us.

I walked slowly next to Malcolm, concern burning a hole in my stomach. "How could those monsters do this? Steal children? I thought they were after me."

Malcolm's heartbeat was strong and steady beside me. I knew he was frustrated, but the leader in him wouldn't let that emotion take over.

"They probably stole them to feed. It takes powerful dark magic to raise the dead, and to *keep* them that way. Sacrificing magical beings will feed the spell animating the shades' corpses. The fact that they're young ones makes the effect more potent."

I shuddered. "So the shades strengthen themselves by killing others. That's sick."

"Yes." His enigmatic gaze cut to me in the dark. "It is. And they've likely done this before. The shades' strength and speed has increased since they surfaced. By now, they're an equal match for me and my brothers, which is something very few supernaturals can boast."

I liked that he was confident enough in himself to be able to admit that—I'd met plenty of guys whose fragile male egos couldn't handle acknowledging any weakness. But I hated to think of how much stronger the shades might become if they continued to sacrifice innocents.

Distracted by my thoughts, I tripped on a rail, stumbling slightly.

Like lightning, Malcolm's hand reached out to steady me. His large, warm fingers closed around my upper arm, and heat zinged through me like I'd been electrified.

My breath caught in my throat, and I heard his hitch too.

Thank God, it's not just me.

The unexpected events of the day had distracted me from my confused feelings about what had happened with Malcolm, but now it all came rushing back. I reached up to rest my hand on his forearm, not sure if I was trying to break his grip or stop him from letting go.

"So, what now?"

My voice was a low whisper, and even I wasn't exactly sure what I was asking. Was I talking about the shades and the missing goblin children? Or about Malcolm and me?

The vampire's warm fingers grasped my chin to tilt my face up. His eyes gleamed like melted chocolate in the dim light, and I pulled my bottom lip between my teeth, trying to keep my pulse even.

"Now, wildcat, would be an excellent time for you to have another vision."

24

WILLOW

TRYING to have a vision when you don't know how to control your own abilities is like trying to make yourself sneeze.

In other words, damn near impossible.

Sol seemed to know more about the gift of Sight than his brothers, but everything he knew was theoretical. He couldn't teach me how to control it; he could only give me vague suggestions of things that might help. And despite their wide network of supernatural connections in the city, none of their friends or acquaintances had this ability either.

It'd been three days since our trek through the subway lines. If I couldn't get something to happen soon, there was talk of taking me to a dark magician and seeing if he could unlock the power I wasn't able to access.

Fear was an excellent motivator, and I was definitely afraid of letting some magic user poke around in my psyche. But even that prospect hadn't been enough to unlock my gift.

My hands lashed out, striking the heavy bag with a quick

whap-whap. I blew out a breath and punched again, dancing around the bag like I'd seen boxers do in movies.

This was the first time I'd dared to return to the training room since Malcolm and I had our encounter down here. He hadn't ever spoken of it to me, and I hadn't said anything to him either—but I knew he thought about it. I felt his heated gaze lingering on me often.

Had he told Jerrett and Sol what happened? God, I hoped not.

Malcolm didn't seem like the type of guy to boast of his conquests, but he was obviously close with his brothers.

Maybe, like Jerrett had said, they *shared.*

A confusing mix of emotions burned through me. How had these men rampaged into my life and transformed it—transformed *me*—so completely? And it wasn't just the mutation from human to vampire. In fact, that was starting to feel like the least of the changes in me.

There was something bigger underneath that. A fundamental, seismic shift in the essence of who I was.

Was this really me?

This woman who acted on impulse, who followed her instincts—who took what she wanted without apology, for no other reason than that she wanted it?

My hands working the heavy bag slowed. I straightened, breathing deeply.

And if it is me... is that really a such a bad thing?

I'd been married for nine years and had spent eight of them trying to convince myself I wasn't miserable. That everything was okay. That asking for more than the meager life I had was selfish and unreasonable.

It'd taken me so long to tell Kyle I wanted a divorce because I'd been afraid of starting over on my own. And, stupidly, I'd been afraid of hurting Kyle. I had put his happiness over my own every day for nine years, even though he'd never done the same for me.

I punched the bag again, harder this time. I hit the same spot over and over, finally letting out years worth of frustration and anger.

And I *was* angry. I'd never really been able to admit it until now, but I was angry at Kyle for relegating me to the back burner for so long—for making me feel worthless. Not because he'd hit me or abused me in any way, but because he'd simply never treated me like I had any worth.

Hell, even the divorce, the thing I'd avoided for so long to spare his feelings, had barely seemed to affect him in any way.

I would never live like that again.

My knuckles split on the bag, and a sharp breath behind me drew my attention. I whirled around as the heavy bag shook and quivered on its chain.

Sol stood in the doorway.

Jesus. You'd think with super hearing, I wouldn't get snuck up on so often.

Then again, I was living with three deadly hunters. No wonder I never heard them coming.

"How long were you watching me?" I asked, then slapped a hand over my mouth. "I mean, not *watching*. I didn't..."

My voice was muffled by my fingers, and I trailed off, unsure what to say.

Nice, Willow. Very socially awkward.

But Sol smiled, his expression warm.

"You can call it watching, but I don't do it with my eyes. I've gotten very good at observing with my other senses. When Fate granted me immortal life, she didn't see fit to return my eyesight.

But she did grant me a sixth sense that helps me function just as well."

Curiosity burned through me. It was probably rude to ask, but I'd wondered about this ability of his ever since I'd met him. "So, how does it work? Can you sense what color my hair is?"

The blond vampire stepped into the room, walking toward me unerringly. He chuckled. "No. Color is a purely visual construct, so I can't tell what color it is. However, I can tell that it's soft, smells of cherry and a hint of spice, and that it's slipping out of the ponytail you pulled it into."

My eyes widened. I touched the loose strand of hair that had indeed fallen from my ponytail, tugging it between my fingers before I tucked it behind my ear. "How?"

"It's hard to describe. It's a combination of so many senses working in concert that it's difficult to break down how the perceptions form in my head. But my sixth sense allows me to 'see' auras of a sort. I can feel energy. It's stronger from living beings and supernaturals, but even inanimate objects give off some energy."

"Holy shit."

Sol's lips quirked up, his light green eyes dancing with humor. "That's one way to put it, yes."

He stopped in front of me and caught my hand in his.

Blood was still smeared across my knuckles, and I didn't miss the way his nostrils flared as he inhaled the scent. For a breathless second, I was convinced he was going to lick the droplets from the back of my hand, and my skin tingled at the thought.

But instead, he led me across the room. I followed willingly, too busy staring at him in amazement to put up any resistance. A small chest of drawers stood by the weapons rack, and he pulled open the top drawer and removed a clean, white cloth.

There was a long silence as Sol gently wiped the blood from my knuckles. I wondered if he could tell I was staring at him. Actually, I was positive he could, but for some reason, that knowledge wasn't enough to stop me.

He was so strikingly handsome it was impossible not to stare. His wavy blond hair formed a widow's peak on his forehead, and not even the florescent lights overhead could dim the glow of his golden skin. His body looked incredible in his well tailored shirt and pants, and he had a fresh scent, spicy and warm.

"There. Good as new."

As Sol finished cleaning my knuckles, I looked down to see that the skin had already healed over.

"I still can't get used to that. The healing thing." I didn't pull my hand from his grasp, and he made no move to release me.

"You will. You have time."

I huffed a laugh. "Good point. As long as those shades don't kill me first."

"They won't. We'll keep you safe. You know that, don't you, Willow tree?"

His grip on my hand tightened until I nodded. He relaxed slightly, finally moving away from me and crossing back toward the door.

"This is a stupid question, I know," he shot back over his shoulder. "But have you had any more visions?"

I sighed, feeling like a dismal failure. "No."

"It's all right. You will."

An unladylike snort burst from my lips as I followed him out the door. I didn't want to linger in the training room. If Malcolm happened to come down here again, I honestly wasn't sure what would happen. Better to avoid the temptation altogether.

"How are you so sure? I might never have a vision again. It could have been a freak thing. A one-off, a total fluke."

"No." Sol preceded me up the stairs to the first floor. "I don't believe that."

"Why not?"

"Because Fate led us to you for a reason. She knew you would help us. She knew we needed you."

His voice softened as he said the last bit, and a thrill ran through me. Trying to shove the butterflies in my stomach back into their cocoons, I snorted. "Yeah, well, Fate might need to kick it up a notch if she's serious about me helping you find those shades. Maybe *she* can send me a vision or something."

"It doesn't work like that," Sol said, slowing so I could walk beside him along the narrow hall.

I wasn't sure if he was leading me or I was leading him at this point. Not that I had anywhere important to go.

Except into a vision. Hopefully soon.

"I know." I ran a finger down the smooth cream-colored wall as we passed. "I just need help. I have no fucking idea what I'm doing."

Sol's sightless eyes flicked my way. "I'm sorry we can't be of more assistance. Your gift is beyond our abilities." His brows furrowed. "What were you doing when you had the first vision?"

I was sure every one of his senses could pick up the wildfire blazing under my skin as I dropped my eyes to the dark hardwood floor. "You... um, you really don't know? Malcolm didn't tell you?"

"Tell me what? All I know is he brought you upstairs to your room before coming to get us. You were out cold, your aura dimmed. Completely unresponsive."

Sol hadn't mentioned anything about my shredded bra or exposed breasts, so I assumed Malcolm had dressed me before he went to get his brothers. I felt a swell of gratitude for the strong, stoic, tortured man. He may have had his own reasons for keeping our encounter from his brothers, but I appreciated that he'd left me with a little bit of my dignity intact.

Of course, that was all about to go out the window now.

Because Sol still had his head cocked toward me, waiting for an answer to his question.

Hoo boy.

"I was… kissing."

"*Kissing?*" His eyebrows shot up toward his perfect hairline, and I wanted to sink into the floor.

"Yes. Malcolm and I were training, and then… things got a little heated. We were on the floor of the training room, and we were"—*doing so much more than*—"kissing, and all of a sudden my soul sort of slipped out of my body. The next thing I knew, I woke up in bed with you sitting next to me."

I finished speaking in a rush, hoping he wouldn't have any probing follow-up questions.

But Sol didn't say anything.

Instead, he stopped in his tracks, holding out a hand to stop me too. I looked over at him hopefully. As embarrassing as it was, maybe my confession had actually triggered something—given him some idea of what it was that had brought on the vision, and how to replicate it.

Before I could ask him, he turned toward me, grabbing my upper arms firmly in his strong hands and pressing my back to the wall.

My pulse spiked at his sudden smooth movement, at the commanding way he controlled my body.

"What... what are you doing?" I whispered.

Sol cupped my cheeks, his palms warm and soft. He tilted my face up gently, gazing down at me with eyes that, though blind, saw more of me than almost any person I'd ever known.

"I'm helping you find your Sight, little Willow tree."

Holding my face perfectly still, he dipped his head and brought his lips to mine.

It wasn't like Malcolm's kiss at all.

That had been desperate and out of control, full of shame and confusion.

This was careful and deliberate, intentional and unapologetic. Sol knew exactly what he was doing. He knew what he wanted. And we wasn't sorry about it.

His lips moved against mine as he took his time tasting me, teasing me. I tried to hold still, to allow this to be a simple experiment, an attempt to bring on the vision and nothing more.

Just like having sex when you're pregnant to bring on labor, I thought wildly. *It's clinical. That's all.*

A sudden image flashed through my head.

Me. Naked. Riding Sol. My hands resting on his chest as I rocked up and down, chasing my pleasure. His sightless gaze locked on me, a look of such worship and lust on his face as he stroked my fevered skin—

My knees buckled.

That hadn't been a real vision—at least, I didn't think so—but the image had been so powerful my clit throbbed and my entire body ached with longing.

Sol's firm grip had kept me from falling, and now I used it to pull him closer to me. I tugged his hands away from my face, guiding them down my body as I wrapped my legs around him.

Without ever breaking the contact of our lips, Sol gave me what I needed. His hands slid around behind me, cupping my ass and lifting me against him in one smooth movement. I felt weightless in his arms, and when he finally broke away from my lips to trail hot kisses down the side of my neck, my head tilted back in ecstasy.

Then I kept tilting.

Just like it had that first time with Malcolm, my soul suddenly seemed to weigh twice as much as my body. My physical form was wrapped in Sol's protective embrace, head tilted up, wide eyes staring at the ceiling. But my soul fell backward, sliding through the wall, through the floor, through layers of rock and sediment into nothing.

For the second time, blackness swallowed me up.

The panic was no less acute, even having been here once before. I had the terrifying feeling that I might get stuck here, trapped in nothingness, trapped *as* nothingness. Floating forever.

Then, slowly, the world coalesced around me.

I hovered in the air, just like I had last time. Below me, the same abandoned structure I'd seen before crouched like a gargoyle in the large field. There were fewer shades than there had been last time, but several still floated around in the dim moonlight outside.

My mind raced. At least we knew they were out of New York. And this place must be their hideout if they'd returned here again. But where was *here*? I needed to find something new, to see something I hadn't before, or this entire trip would be wasted.

Gathering my focus, I fought to move my consciousness through space. It was like trying to swim with no arms, and for a moment, nothing happened.

I stopped, frustration rising in me.

Damn it. Maybe the problem is that I'm still trying to move as if I have limbs. I don't. So flailing won't make a bit of difference.

But how did creatures with no limbs move?

Feeling a little ridiculous, I imagined my consciousness as a snake wending its way through the grass. An effortless, undulating glide forward.

Elation filled me when the old building in the distance seemed to grow. It was getting closer! Or rather, I was getting closer to it. I kept up the careful glide, watching the shades to make sure they truly couldn't see me.

But no heads turned my way, even as I slipped through a large broken window and into the abandoned building.

It *was* a church.

Only about half the pews remained intact; the rest had rotted away or lay amongst small piles of debris scattered about the room. A large cross hung on a wall at the back of the church. On the dais beneath it sat an altar stained with something thick, dark, and matte. Dried blood.

Then a faint sound reached me.

Crying.

A child was crying.

I searched the rest of the large space. On the choir risers off to the side of the dais, a cluster of small bodies huddled together. The brownish-gray color of their skin confirmed they were goblins.

Fear lanced through me. How many of them were there? How many had died already?

I tried to move forward again, but in my panic, I lost the easy glide I'd found before. I struggled against empty space, but it was no good. Instead of moving forward, my consciousness was tugged back, out through the window where I'd come in.

No! *No, no, no*!

Scrabbling for some kind of purchase in the ether, I tried to slow my movement. I couldn't go yet. I needed to find something. Some kind of landmark or clue. *Something*!

But I was flying backward, gliding away so fast the thick, dense forest below me was almost a blur.

Then I saw it. Heard it.

The roar of rushing rapids.

The white spray as thousands of gallons of water hurtled over a sheer cliff face.

Niagara Falls.

Well, that'll do for a landmark.

25

SOL

"YOU'RE TOO TENSE, MY BOY." Yuliya clucked her tongue. "She'll be fine. She's hearty, this girl. Too skinny, but hearty."

"I know she is, Yuliya. And I know she will be."

But that didn't unwind the knot of worry in my stomach. I'd felt Willow clinging to me before her spirit left her body, and the urge to hold on to her, to protect her no matter what, had been more powerful than I'd ever experienced.

I had kissed her to try to provoke a vision, and to prove a point to myself—though what that point was, I no longer quite remembered. If it'd been to prove I wasn't under her thrall the same way my brothers were, my plan had backfired entirely. Because as soon as my lips touched hers, I'd been lost completely.

There was something so alluring about Willow.

Several things actually.

There was her softness and innocence in a world that tried its best to foster disillusionment. There was the steel backbone that hid underneath her sweetness—the bravery and stubbornness that glowed inside her like a fire on a dark night. Her enchanting cherry-almond scent. Her smooth skin, beautiful despite the markings cruelly carved into her body. Her ass, which fit so perfectly in the palms of my hands.

I shifted uncomfortably. The need to finish what we'd started left my cock semi-hard, but now wasn't the time to think about that. Willow was laid out on the bed again, her breath so shallow and slow that I could barely sense it. She felt almost dead.

A shock of panic ran through me at that thought, and I reached out to grip her soft, delicate-fingered hand. Her skin was reassuringly warm, and I raised her palm to my lips, pressing a kiss to the center of it.

I couldn't help but inhale her essence one more time, like a junky getting high. The sweet, natural scent of her skin and blood.

And beneath it, something more.

Some scent, some taste I couldn't identify. It was familiar, but just out of my mind's reach. And it drew me like a siren's song.

"Stop sniffing her hand and let her rest!"

Yuliya smacked the back of my head lovingly—and hard.

I let out a defeated chuckle and gently replaced Willow's hand on the bedspread. Yuliya was one of the only people I knew who would give powerful vampires like my brothers and me so much sass. It was why we'd hired her, and why we all adored her. None of us had wanted a housekeeper who tiptoed around the place, jumping at our every move.

Yuliya didn't tiptoe. And she definitely didn't jump.

She *had* gone after Jerrett with a broom several times, threatening to wallop him. But he had absolutely deserved it.

"She is a lucky girl, my boy. To have three people care about her as you and your brothers do."

The old witch's voice had turned serious, and I tipped my

head up to regard her. Her heartbeat was strong but fast, and the skin of her hands sounded like paper as she twisted her fingers together.

"Four people, I think." I smiled up at her, and she clucked again.

"I do like her. She is good for you. All of you."

Before I could respond to that, Willow gasped. Her body sprang up off the bed, her hand grasping desperately for mine. I tugged her quickly into the comfort of my embrace, expecting the same panic and disorientation as last time.

But Willow, as if she'd heard Yuliya and me talking while she slept, demonstrated once again how strong she was.

Though her body still quaked with tremors and her heartbeat was a rapid staccato beat in her chest, her voice was strong when she said, "I know where the shades are hiding, Sol. The kids are there—some of them still alive. We have to help them."

As it turned out, Willow didn't know exactly where they were. But she'd seen enough for us to figure out the rest.

A few moments after she woke, Jerrett and Malcolm arrived in the room. Malcolm's voice echoed with suspicion when he asked what had brought on the second vision. Mine was full of challenge when I told him.

I could sense Willow blushing furiously next to me, but I caught the scent of something else too.

Arousal.

Hers, and my own. My brothers' too.

It was time to stop tiptoeing around the feelings we all shared for her. Malcolm may not be ready to admit it—and I understood why, even though his own actions toward her made him a hypocrite—but she was ours. She owned us and had since the night we turned her.

Willow had described her vision for us several times, going through everything in painstaking detail. When she'd reached the part where she flew away from the church and past the rushing water of Niagara Falls, Jerrett had grunted under his breath. He'd typed away on his phone for several seconds and then let out a triumphant noise.

If we assumed Willow's spirit traveled toward her body when it left the site of the ruin, and we knew she'd passed over a large forest before she saw the waterfalls, that narrowed down the possible location of the shades significantly.

They were in Canada, not far from the border.

"Are you sure you're right about this?"

Willow's voice broke me from my thoughts. The sweet, melodic tone was tinged with worry. She'd been anxious and jittery ever since she woke up.

"As sure as we can be," Jerrett tossed back from the driver's seat. "We'll be able to pinpoint their exact location once we get closer. As long as we're right about the general area, we can track them."

"Okay." She blew out a breath, her body relaxing beside me—but only slightly. "How long will it take to get there?"

"About five hours." I punched the back of Jerrett's seat lightly. "But with the way my brother drives, probably closer to four."

"Pshh. You love the way I drive."

"Let's just say it's one of the few things that makes me glad I can't see," I shot back, chuckling.

"Are you all—?" Willow broke off, smoothing down her hair.

Hoping conversation would ease some of her anxiousness, I pulled her hand into mine and squeezed. "Are we what?"

She hesitated for a moment, but like it usually did with her, curiosity won out. "Are you all actually brothers? I always hear you say that, but... well, I don't know if you know this, but you guys don't look anything alike."

Jerrett howled with laughter, and even Malcolm chuckled.

"Yeah, did you know that, Sol? Sorry to break it to you, but my devastating good looks are all mine," Jerrett teased.

"At least my face isn't so boring I had to decorate it with a bunch of metal just to spruce it up a little," I shot back lightly.

Willow giggled. "Calm down, boys. You're all very sexy."

Jerrett's voice dropped, turning smooth and rich. "Hear that? She thinks I'm sexy."

Willow sucked in a breath beside me, embarrassment setting in as she realized what she'd said. She tried to reclaim her hand, but I didn't let her, resting it on my thigh and squeezing tighter.

"She said we *all* are, jackass. Not just you." Malcolm punched our brother's arm, more lighthearted than I'd seen him in a long time.

I turned to Willow. "To answer your question—no. Though we may act like it sometimes, we're not brothers born of the same mother. But we *are* brothers in all the ways that count."

"Brothers in all the ways that count," she repeated with a soft sigh. "I like that. I never had any siblings, and I always felt like I was missing out on something amazing."

I rubbed my thumb across the back of her hand, reveling in the little shiver that worked its way through her body at my touch. "You can build your own family, Willow. You can make it anything you want."

This time, she was the one to tighten her grip on me. "Thanks,

Sol." She paused. "So, have you all known each other a long time?"

"A very long time." Malcolm's voice was serious.

"Which one of you is oldest?"

I was enjoying this side of Willow. Curious as a kitten, open and earnest. I could tell my brothers did too, as a happy energy filled the car.

"What, can't you tell?" Jerrett drummed a rhythm on the steering wheel, still chuckling.

She shook her head, and the scent of almond wafted from her thick hair.

"Guess," he prodded.

I felt her gaze shift to each of us in turn—could sense the intensity of her stare as she regarded me.

"Sol," she said finally.

Jerrett cracked up again. "Nope! Try again, Will."

"Malcolm?"

"Ohh, so close, but no cigar. I'll let you have one more guess though."

"*You*?"

Incredulity resonated in her voice, and this time Malcolm and I laughed.

"Jerrett is almost two thousand years old," I murmured. "Hard to believe, isn't it?"

"Yeah, kind of." Her voice was low, as if she worried she might offend him. "He seems so… so…"

"Well assimilated?"

"Yeah. He looks so cool. Contemporary. The first time I met him, I thought he was a rock star or something."

Jerrett gave a low, hungry growl. "Damn right, you did, sweetheart."

Willow's breath caught, and the scent of arousal filled the car just like it had the bedroom earlier. I clenched my jaw. We needed to release this tension sooner rather than later. If we didn't, it would keep torturing and distracting us—and for hunters like us, distractions could prove deadly.

"So who's the youngest?" Willow asked, her voice a little rougher than usual as she fought to tamp down her body's response.

"I am."

Her head whipped toward me. "What? Really?"

"Yes. I'm only a hundred and fifty-five years old. I was fighting for the North in the Civil War when I became gravely ill. Lupus, although I didn't know that at the time. I lost my eyesight and would've lost my life, but Jerrett turned me before death took me."

"Holy shit!"

A grin tugged at my lips. "That is one way to put it."

Her voice grew pensive. "Wow. You fought in the Civil War. One hundred and fifty-five years ago. And Jerrett… two *thousand* years? Holy fuck. That's so long. This is all just… I mean, I *knew*, but…"

She trailed off, sounding lost.

I reached over with my other hand and cupped the side of her cheek. A tear landed on my fingertip, and I was struck by the strangest urge to lift it to my mouth, as if by drinking her tears I could take her sadness upon myself.

"You won't be alone, Willow. You'll live many, many years; but I promise, you'll never be alone."

Willow gave a watery chuckle, leaning into my touch. "I came to New York to re-invent myself. I just never thought the new me would be so crazily different from the old me."

"I don't think she is." Malcolm spoke quietly from the front seat. "I think this is who you've always been. You just didn't let your true self free before."

There was a moment of heavy silence, then Willow's shoulders shifted as she pulled in a deep breath. I felt her muscles relax, and she leaned her head against my shoulder.

Malcolm was right.

This was the real Willow, the one Fate had always intended her to be. She was meant for more than a shitty marriage in a boring life. Her light was meant to shine brighter than that.

And as her body molded to mine, her head tilting so she could gaze out the window beside us, I knew she was beginning to accept that truth.

Good girl. I brought our joined hands to my lips and kissed her knuckles. *There's strength in fighting, but there's strength in giving in too.*

26

WILLOW

THE DARK SCENERY of New York state whizzed by as Jerrett's Mercedes sped down the road. I didn't let go of Sol's hand, and when his arm found its way around my shoulders, I burrowed into his embrace.

It was strange to feel so safe and protected with these men whom most of the world would've seen as a threat. And they *were* dangerous, of that I had no doubt. But I also knew on an almost instinctual level that they would never do anything to hurt me, never put me in danger if they could help it.

The only danger they presented to me was to my heart.

And that danger was very real.

I don't mind sharing.

Jerrett's words wouldn't stop playing through my mind. His implication had been very clear—hell, he'd basically come right out and said it. He wanted me. And if Sol and Malcolm did too, he'd share. Could I share, though? Could I share myself with three men and give enough to each of them?

And why the hell was I even thinking about three when I

wasn't sure it was a good idea to get involved with even *one* of them?

The conversation drifted to other topics as we drove. I told them a bit more about my life in Ohio and what had brought me to New York. The temperature in the car dropped several degrees when I mentioned that after our second anniversary, Kyle had suggested we stop celebrating them—ostensibly to "save money."

"But we never did anything with the money we saved," I added, shaking my head. "It probably just bought him more beer and potato chips."

"Where does this guy live?"

Jerrett's voice was so fierce that for a moment, fear skittered up my spine.

"In… Cincinnati." I didn't give more details than that, although I was sure an expert hunter like him would have no problem tracking down my ex. "But it doesn't matter anymore. He's out of my life now. And he wasn't all that bad. He wasn't abusive or anything. He never hit me."

"That's the lowest fucking bar I've ever heard of," Jerrett growled. "The man let a gorgeous rose wither on the vine, and I'm supposed to give him credit because he didn't take a pair of clippers to it? Nope, sorry, sweetheart."

Another emotion mingled with my concern. Something more powerful and much sweeter. Still, I had to make sure Jerrett didn't do something stupid just for me.

"I'm not making excuses for Kyle. But please don't do anything to him. I can take care of myself now. And I'd rather you use your hunting abilities on the creatures that really deserve it." I thought of the shades in that abandoned church, the blood dripping down the altar. "Feel free to rip *them* to shreds."

"Oh, I plan to, Will."

Moonlight glinted off Jerrett's lip ring, and his grin in the rearview mirror was bloodthirsty.

A few hours later, he pulled off onto a small side road and parked the car. Everyone piled out. I followed, glancing around in confusion.

"We're not there yet, are we? Why did we stop?"

"The Canadian border doesn't mean jack to supernaturals. Vampires are loosely divided by continent, with our king ruling over all of North America. But if we try to enter Canada through the human routes, human rules will apply. Do you have a passport?" Jerrett pressed a button on his key fob to lock the car.

I blinked. "Oh. No. I totally forgot about that."

Sol smiled. "Luckily, you won't need it."

"Why not?"

"Because we're going to shadow run the rest of the way."

Right. Duh. It made sense that vampires wouldn't get around the same old boring way humans did.

"Don't we still have a pretty long way to go though?"

"Yes. But we can run fast. We'll show you how—you've already got the basics of shadow running down, so it should be easy enough for you to pick up," Malcolm said, stretching his arms over his head.

I didn't blame him. His large, muscled frame had to have been a little cramped in Jerrett's car.

"When you get a good head of steam going, the shadows pretty much pull you along. It's not actually teleporting, but it's the next best thing." Jerrett raised his eyebrows temptingly at me. "Are you ready to fly, sweetheart?"

~

FLYING.

That was an excellent word for it.

Flitting from shadow to shadow with the brothers, running so fast my feet barely touched the ground, I did feel like I was airborne. We covered miles in mere minutes, and despite how fast we were going, I didn't feel winded. I felt exhilarated. Exuberant.

At least, until Malcolm slowed, raising his fist in the air to signal the rest of us to follow his lead. Then my exuberance faded quickly, my stomach sinking like a rock as I remembered why we were doing this.

I caught a hint of stale blood on the breeze, and a chill washed over my skin.

We were close.

My gaze flicked between the three brothers, watching them silently communicate. Malcolm jerked his head, and we veered slightly to the right, walking through the woods on silent feet.

A part of me still couldn't believe they'd agreed to let me come. They could've taken the information I'd given them from my vision and left me in the house with Yuliya. Hell, they could've tied me to the bed again.

But they hadn't.

I appreciated that as protective as they were, they didn't treat me like a helpless fawn.

Now I just had to prove to them, and myself, that I wasn't one.

The trees here were dense and thick, blocking out most of the moonlight from above. What little made it through the foliage flickered across the ground in odd patterns that seemed to undulate like living things.

I swallowed.

Stop creeping yourself out, Willow. There are enough real *monsters out there to be afraid of; don't make up new ones.*

But I couldn't keep my heart from thudding heavily in my chest as we walked. The men could definitely hear it, and I hated that they knew I was scared.

A few minutes later, Sol made a low sound and gestured to the left. He changed course slightly, brushing the trunks of the trees we passed with his fingertips as he moved confidently through the forest.

When the woods began to thin, the scent of blood hanging in the air grew stronger. My stomach roiled even as my mouth watered. This blood didn't smell like the bagged stuff the brothers kept in their fridge. It was different than the human blood I'd smelled all around me that night at the club. But it was definitely fresh.

A clearing opened up, and I recognized the sight before us. The church from my vision loomed in the darkness, bigger in real life than I'd expected. It dominated the landscape, a hulking structure of rotting wood and stained glass. It was like the skeleton of a once beautiful building, hollowed out and empty—but the bones were still strong enough to stand.

No shades roamed the clearing like they had in my vision, but the lingering stench of rot and decay made me certain they'd been here recently.

I bit my lip, all the courage draining from my body like someone had poked a hole in me.

A large, rough hand cupped the back of my neck. I'd pulled my hair up into a tight bun to keep it out of the way, but a few tendrils had escaped and tickled my skin as Malcolm gave a gentle squeeze. He stood beside me, his gaze fixed on the church ahead of us.

"You can do this, wildcat. You've got a hunter's instincts."

I wanted to thank him, but I was afraid my voice would crack if I spoke. So I just nodded, keeping my eyes trained forward too.

Sol stepped into the lead, tipping his head up slightly as if tasting the wind. I couldn't even imagine the array of sensory input he was processing.

His brain must work at lightning speed.

Like a true predator.

He shook his head, and that must've been what the others were waiting for, because they crept after him on silent feet. I hung behind Malcolm, with Jerrett behind me. Even as they focused on the hunt, I could tell they were watching out for me, making sure someone had my back at all times.

I liked that feeling.

A low, wide staircase led up to the front entrance of the church. A set of large double doors stood ajar, one of them broken and sagging off its hinges. There was just enough space for us to slip inside without moving the doors, but we could only pass through one by one.

Sol entered first and gave a low call to let us know it was clear. We squeezed in after him.

The inside of the church wasn't much darker than the outside. The nearly full moon was visible through a hole in the ceiling by the door, and several of the large stained glass windows had been broken. The ones that were still intact cast patterns of strange, muted colors across the mildewed floor.

I blinked, staring toward the front of the church. The large cross on the wall was visible in the darkness, but I could barely make out an altar below it. I knew it was there though. The smell of blood had grown even more pungent when we'd stepped into the enclosed space.

"No sign of the shades." Jerrett's whisper was little more than a breath, but it still seemed loud in the heavy silence.

"Up front. That's where the goblin kids were," I murmured, stepping forward.

I traversed the debris-littered floor quickly, my vampire grace and eyesight miraculously keeping me from tripping over anything.

But when I reached the choir risers, my heart sank.

"There's no one here. Damn it."

"Don't panic yet." Malcolm's voice was strong and steady, like a balm on my nerves. "They may have just moved."

I swallowed. *Right.* They could still be here somewhere. They could still be alive.

"Hello? Is anybody there?" I kept my voice hushed as I called out into the darkness. If the shades were here, they'd probably already heard us, but I saw no reason to draw more attention to ourselves than necessary.

A small sound made its way back to me. A rustling, scratching noise. Probably just rats or mice who'd made their home in this old, abandoned building.

Still, I pulled the hefty metal flashlight Jerrett had given me earlier from my belt. It had struck me as a little funny that vampires would need flashlights, but now I was grateful I had it. My vision was a dozen times better than it had been when I was human, but it wasn't like I had infrared sight or anything. The darkest shadows were still impenetrable to my eyes.

I flicked the switch, and a small, concentrated beam of white light hit the church wall. I panned it around, aiming it under pews and behind piles of wood and moldy cloth. When it illuminated the altar like a spotlight, I gagged. The blood had been nearly dried in my vision, but now it glistened in the light, shining bright red.

"That's new. Fresh. Recent." My jaw clenched around the words, and they came out clipped and harsh.

"I know." Malcolm's voice was grim.

The noise came again, and the flashlight beam jerked as I chased the sound. A pair of wide brown eyes blinked in the bright light.

"There! On the dais!"

I darted forward, the flashlight bouncing in my hand as I ran. I cleared the stairs up to the dais in two large steps, and crouched down on the corner of the raised platform. Seven or eight small bodies were pressed together in a clump against the wall, as if they could somehow force the ancient wood to absorb them.

The one who peered up at me had a round, squashed face, with gray-brown skin and pointed ears. He made a small noise, and several of the others tugged him back down, shushing him.

"It's okay." My voice shook, but I tried to make it sound soothing instead of panicked. "I'm not going to hurt you. I'm here to help."

"They can't understand you." Jerrett came up beside me, his brow furrowed. "And I don't speak goblin."

"Are they dangerous?" I peered down at the mass of huddled bodies, pity filling my chest.

"Nah. You saw the ones in the subway. Not even the adults are that dangerous. The kids—no way."

"Good. We have to get them out of here."

"I don't like this." Sol stood in the aisle between the pews, just in front of the dais. "It's too quiet. Where are the shades? They were here in both of your other visions."

"I don't know. But I'm sure wherever they are, they won't be gone long. We need to hurry."

Switching the flashlight to my left hand, I used my right hand to prod the lump of bodies before me. I found a little fist with rough gray-brown skin and tugged on it.

The goblin child resisted at first, but when I pulled a little harder, he peeled away from his friends and glommed onto me instead, wrapping his arms tightly around my leg. I had no idea how old he was, but he only stood about two feet tall.

Another little hand reached out from the pile and grabbed onto him. One of his friends wrapped her arms around his waist. A second later, two more kids had latched onto my other leg. As the pile on the floor dwindled, they stood up faster, until I was surrounded by clinging goblin children.

I looked up at Jerrett to find him watching me with an amused smile. His high cheekbones and long, straight nose looked even sharper in the harsh shadows, and his eyes glinted with humor.

"What?" I shrugged awkwardly. "I'm good with kids."

"I can see that. Good thing too, 'cause I can't imagine they'd take to Mal like that. Or me."

"Help me get them out."

I staggered forward, my movements hampered by the kids attached to my legs. We made our way slowly down the stairs and toward the front entrance, the three brothers keeping a lookout and moving large pieces of debris out of the way.

None of the goblin children made a peep, and I shuddered to think what kind of fear could make kids be *that* quiet.

When we reached the front doors, I put my shoulder against the old wood and pushed hard. With a loud screech that raised the hair on the back of my neck, it moved.

But I stopped in my tracks.

Just like in my vision, several shades drifted through the clearing outside the church. As I watched, two more emerged from the tree line.

Something else drew my eye. Deeper in the forest, so far away I could barely make them out, stood two other figures. Their pale white faces contrasted with the darkness around them, and they tilted their heads to the side in unison, their gazes locked on me.

What on earth?

They were… women. I couldn't tell anything else from this distance, but the delicate features were definitely feminine. Were they who the shades answered to?

That thought was driven from my mind as the shade closest to the church's entrance looked up, its dark gaze landing on me.

A sharp shriek rose from its throat, and it rushed forward, followed by its brethren.

27

JERRETT

"Oh fuck!"

Willow's voice was high and panicked. At any other time, I'd have loved to hear those words come out of her mouth—what was it about a beautiful woman swearing like a sailor that was so damn hot?—but the fear in her tone turned my blood to ice.

"Willow, what the—?"

"Back! Go back!"

She stumbled backward, nearly tripping over the little goblin kids that still clung like leeches to her legs. As she moved out of the way, I saw what'd spooked her. Half a dozen shades raced up the church steps toward us.

Motherfucking shit goddamnit.

"Mal! Sol! Incoming!" I yelled.

Willow crouched, picking up a little body in each arm as my brothers raced past us toward the open door, pulling it shut with a screech of rusty hinges just as the first shade reached it. The creature slammed into it so hard the whole back wall shook. It wasn't like the building was impenetrable—there were gaping holes where half the windows used to be—but this bought us a few seconds to get ready for battle.

Another kid scrambled onto Willow's back, and she looked up at me with wide eyes. "Help me!"

Damn it.

Kids really didn't like me.

Whatever. A goblin bite likely wouldn't be the worst injury I'd sustain tonight. I swept up the remaining rug rats, wrapping my arms around them in a bundle and pinning them to my chest. One little face got trapped right next to mine, wide brown eyes staring at me as I jerked my head to Willow.

"No time to get them out. We need to get them out of the way of the fight!"

She nodded, and we darted toward a little office near the entrance of the church. I kicked the door open, barely breaking my stride as I ran into the room. A plume of dust rose up to greet us, and the little goblin face in front of mine coughed right on me.

Fucking gross.

The office was small, with a little desk, a chair, and several large filing cabinets. Nothing in this room would keep these kids safe if the shades decided to come after them, but I was hoping they wouldn't—not with a much more obvious threat present. The best we could do was make sure the goblin young didn't end up as collateral damage.

Shouts and shrieks echoed from the main church hall.

Guess the shades found a new way in already.

Heart slamming against my ribs in anticipation of the fight, I deposited my load in a corner next to the desk. "Here!"

Willow passed her kids off to me, and I set them down with the others. They all melded together again into one large clinging, amorphous mass, except for the first one Will had picked up. He didn't want to let her go, and I honestly couldn't blame the kid.

She crouched down beside him while I shoved a heavy metal file cabinet toward the desk, making a little cubby for the kids in the corner. It wasn't much, but it was all I could do.

"Here. Take this." Willow pressed the flashlight into the goblin kid's tiny hands. I was sure he didn't understand a single thing she'd said, but he clung to the heavy metal rod like it was a sword. Then he crouched down in front of his group of huddled friends, his face terrified but determined.

Damn. My kind of kid.

I grabbed Willow's arm and pulled her away. Part of me wanted to make her stay under the desk with the rug rats, but I figured my chances of getting that to happen were about as good as getting her to sprout wings so she could fly away.

Whatever doubts she might have about herself, Willow wasn't the type to shy away from danger when something she cared about was on the line.

I peeked through the open doorway. Outside, my brothers fought several shades at once. Or maybe "kept them occupied" was a better way to put it. Between the two of them, they kept the shades engaged, but they were outnumbered too badly to go on the offensive. I needed to get out there and help them.

"Let's go!" I whispered.

Will cast one last glance back at the kids then nodded.

We crept out of the room quietly. I closed the door and wedged a large splinter of wood between it and the frame, blocking it closed.

Mal let out an angry cry as one of the shades got in a lucky swipe, opening a gash in his arm.

"Malcolm!"

Willow's pained shout echoed in the church, and for a moment, everything seemed to pause. My brothers and the shades all stopped, their attention drawn to us.

Then two of the dark creatures leapt straight for Willow.

"Oh, no you don't, motherfucker!" I sprang forward, meeting one in midair and driving it backward. Sol leapt after the other.

Before we hit the floor, the creature beneath me evaporated, its body becoming as incorporeal as mist. I rolled sideways, barely avoiding getting my head stomped on as the shade jumped to its feet and became solid again.

Shit. Strength and speed were usually a vampire's greatest advantages in a fight, but these damn shades matched us on both counts. What the fuck were they?

The thing dove for me, but I kicked out with both feet, launching it up and over my body. It flew through the aisle, landing in a black heap near the stairs leading up to the dais. I ripped a plank of wood off the back of a rotting pew and raced forward.

When the thing stood, I hit it with everything I had. The wood splintered into fragments and the shade screeched, collapsing onto the stairs. It crawled up them, its body flickering in and out of solidity. I must've stunned it.

Gritting my teeth, I strode forward, grabbing the shade by the back of the head and dragging it up to the dais. Its hair was stringy, almost slippery, and I could feel it trying to fade away. Not giving it a chance, I hauled it up to the large blood-covered altar under the cross and bashed its head against the stone—once, twice, three times. And a few more for good measure.

The shade let out a gurgling cry that cut off in a sharp grunt.

Its body began to shrivel up, shrinking and drying out until all that remained was a mummified corpse.

Runes marked the gray skin of this one, just like the other.

Just like Willow.

Snarling, I kicked the corpse out of the way, turning to rejoin the fight. Another desiccated body lay sprawled across a pile of broken wood. Willow and my brothers faced off with two more in the corner near the office.

Fuck.

Were they still trying to get to the kids?

"Mal! Get ready for me!"

I was already running as I called his name, and he whipped his head around, catching sight of me. The shade he fought kept going incorporeal, evading his blows. But as my brother dropped his hands, letting his guard down, it sensed his distraction. Rearing up, it solidified to go in for the kill.

Too fucking late.

Without slowing down, I grabbed a piece of jaggedly broken pipe from a pile on the floor and launched myself off the back of the last pew. I drove the sharp pipe straight through the shade's back as I came down, breaking its spine with a loud crunch.

The thing didn't even make a noise as it died.

"Nice." I stood, ripping the piece of pipe from dried flesh. "You really sold that 'incompetence' bit. Thanks for keeping this fucker distracted."

He chuckled darkly. "These things obviously aren't used to working in teams. It's the only reason we haven't lost this fight yet."

"Speaking of working in teams!" Sol called. "Little help?"

He and the remaining shade traded blows right outside the

door to the office. Will was stationed protectively in front of the door, wielding a large metal candlestick like a baseball bat.

At least she hadn't jumped on this shade's back like the one outside her apartment. Not that I didn't respect the fuck out of her fighting spirit, but I wasn't sure my heart could take her constantly throwing herself at danger like that.

I shot a glance at Mal. "Only one left. Should be a piece of cake, right?"

"Only one at the moment. There were more in both of Willow's visions—and I haven't seen any armless shades here, have you? More of these things are out there somewhere."

I scowled at him as we raced toward Sol and the shade. "Goddamn it. Thanks a lot, Debbie Downer."

He grabbed the creature and pulled it away from Sol, spinning it around. "Take it out on this."

I smirked. "With fucking pleasure."

Swinging the metal pipe in a wide arc, I caught the shade across the face. Viscous black fluid flew from the wound as the thing gargled in pain. It went incorporeal a second later, darting right toward me, then through me. Before I could pivot, cold arms locked around me from behind. Cool liquid dripped down the back of my neck.

"Damn it! This undead motherfucker is bleeding on me!"

I twisted in its grasp, but the thing was as strong as me, and its arm was locked tight around my neck. My brothers advanced slowly, and behind them, Willow watched with wide eyes. I wanted to tell her not to worry—we'd gotten out of way more fucked up situations than this. Mal and Sol had my back. I'd be fine.

But I couldn't tell her shit. The creature was cutting off my air supply.

I couldn't say a fucking word.

Not even a word of warning as a new shade slipped through the large hole in the ceiling near the office, dropping to the floor right next to Willow.

I could only watch in horror as it knocked the weapon out of her hand and grabbed her roughly, enveloping her in darkness.

28

WILLOW

FEAR PUNCHED a hole in my chest as I wriggled in the cold arms wrapped tightly around me.

One second, I'd been watching the brothers fight the final shade. Then Jerrett's eyes, such a clear blue I could see them even in the dark church, had locked on me. The terror in them had scared me shitless, because until that moment, I'd never seen Jerrett look anything but cocky and confident.

His fear wasn't for himself. He'd been afraid for me.

And now I was too.

I had stupidly let my guard slip. I'd been focused on the fight in front of me, intent on keeping the shade out of the small office where the children hid. I hadn't realized, though maybe I should have, that when the shades kept charging the office door, they weren't after the goblin kids—they were after me.

The new shade had appeared out of nowhere, stealing my makeshift club before I even had a chance to swing it. Now I was wrapped so tightly in its grip that all I could see was blackness. All I could smell was death and decayed flesh.

I dug my elbows into the monster's side, dimly aware of three deep male voices shouting my name in panic. I tried to kick, to get some traction against the floor to slow us down, but the shade was taller than me. My feet couldn't find any purchase.

Gasping for air and gagging with each breath, I tried to pull together my scattered thoughts.

Are we... moving in circles?

I struggled to free my head from the shadow creature's crushing grip. Shit. We *were* going in circles. In a spiral, actually, up a winding staircase. Below us, crashes and grunts echoed in the empty church.

"Willllllow!" Jerrett bellowed.

For a second, my panic eased. He was okay, at least. If he could yell like that, the shade must not have him in a chokehold anymore.

But he was still so far away. They all were.

We finally stopped spiraling upward, and I was thrown roughly to the floor in a small room with a large bell suspended in the middle of it. I hit the wooden floor hard, and before I could even turn over, the creature was on me. A bite of pain stung the back of my neck.

Its claws?

No. A knife.

This thing was going to finish whatever job its friend had started that first night.

Summoning all my vampire strength, I heaved my body upward. It worked. The shade was jostled off me, and I darted back toward the stairs. But before I could get far, something heavy hit the back of my head. I went down, my ears ringing as pain surged through my skull.

This time the sting of the knife wasn't as strong—it had to

compete with my other wounds for attention, and my body couldn't process all the sensations at once.

Warm blood trickled across my skin as the creature began adding to the patterns etched on my body. I was still weak and disoriented, but the sound of footsteps on the stairs gave me hope.

My men are coming.

As strange as that thought was—they weren't my men... were they?—it kept my body fighting. I dragged myself forward on my forearms as the shade's weight bore down on me.

Malcolm entered the bell tower first, his face set in a vengeful mask like a god of rage. Sol and Jerrett were right behind him, their handsome features hardly recognizable as they snarled at the shade, revealing their fangs.

The creature stopped carving my skin. It kept its weight on my lower back but hauled my head up by the hair, its claws digging into the tight bun I'd made earlier. The carving knife pressed viciously into the side of my throat, just under my ear, drawing blood.

No one spoke, but the threat was crystal clear.

The men stopped moving, hanging back by the doorway. I could barely see them through the tears swimming in my eyes, but I could feel the morass of emotions churning within them.

My own feelings rose up to match the intensity of theirs.

Disappointment in myself for being the weak link on this makeshift team. Anger at the shades and whoever was behind them for their relentless pursuit of me, for their willingness to sacrifice young, innocent lives for their own gain. Regret that I hadn't had the guts to claim these brothers like I'd wanted to, to mark them as mine and let them mark me. Sorrow that after everything they'd done to save me, these beautiful, terrifying, perfect men would be forced to watch me die.

I wished desperately for some way out of this, begging Fate to intervene. Sol had said she brought me to them for a reason. She couldn't let it end now, could she?

My heart stuttered in my chest as the piercing pressure on my neck eased suddenly. *Is the knife disappearing?*

No. I was.

The knife remained as solid as ever, but like a breath of warm air on a cold night, *I* was evaporating. The strangest sensation filled me as I slowly became incorporeal. It was like turning into smoke. I didn't sink through the floor as I had when falling into visions, but I suddenly couldn't feel the shade's weight on me at all.

Recovering from my shock, I rolled quickly to the side, passing *through* the dark creature and scrambling to my feet a short distance away. I caught a brief sight of three stunned faces, then the men attacked. They dove for the shade, but it followed my lead, becoming incorporeal before any of their blows could land.

Mal bared his teeth in anger, snarling at the monster. But there was nothing the brothers could do. Not until the thing became solid again.

The shade stalked toward me, its massive, shadowy form slightly transparent in this state.

A sudden thought froze my blood.

We were both in the same state. Could it touch me now?

I backed away quickly, but not fast enough. The shade swiped out, raking a clawed hand across my chest. A breathy grunt fell from my lips as I watched the razor-tipped claws pass harmlessly through me.

Guess that answers that question.

But I couldn't attack the shade either. We were at an impasse like this. And it would never let me walk away peacefully. The thing crowded me, hovering so close I could've sworn I felt it brush against me.

"Hey! Get the fuck away from her!" Jerrett's voice was thick with anger.

Steeling myself, I charged through the creature and ran to the other end of the tower, but the shadow monster was on me a minute later. Shit. We could do this all night.

"We need to make it go corporeal," Sol said grimly.

How had they done that before?

Oh, right.

Malcolm had pretended to drop his guard so Jerrett could attack.

"Guys! I'm going to make it shift!"

My voice sounded strange like this, ghostly and faint. But I knew they heard me, because they all shook their heads in unison.

"No, wildcat! You're safe where you are. Stay like that."

Malcolm's voice was firm and commanding. If I'd been one of his brothers, a trained fighter used to following orders from my leader, maybe I would've listened. But I wasn't. I was a scared shitless incorporeal vampire who knew only one way to get us out of this mess.

I honestly wasn't sure how to become solid again. It wasn't like there was some muscle I could flex. So I just focused on the end result I wanted, willing it to work.

It did.

And then several things happened at once.

I became solid.

The shade screeched, becoming corporeal almost at the same moment.

My vampire protectors lunged forward, but the shade pivoted, slashing out with the wicked dagger it still held. It caught Jerrett in the side, and a fountain of blood welled.

"Jerrett!"

The scream tore from my throat even as the shadow creature leapt for me again, wrapping an arm around me.

This time, I didn't go incorporeal. Using a trick Malcolm had taught me, I spun into the shade's movement, redirecting it to the side as I grabbed for the knife. The shade was bigger and much heavier than me, but I had momentum on my side. I shoved, and the creature moved backward a few steps, stumbling toward the large bell hanging over a hole in the center of the room.

Its foot slipped off the edge, stepping into the black abyss. Its head cracked against the giant metal bell with a sickening, dull ringing sound.

And then it fell through the opening, its arms still clutching me.

We plummeted through the darkness together, and my stomach rushed up into my throat. I grappled for the knife, the shade's claws gouging my flesh as we fought for control. Just before we landed, I grabbed the hilt with both hands and twisted the knife toward the shade's chest.

The impact was like getting hit by a car. It ricocheted through me, sending pain radiating through my bones.

For several long moments, I couldn't move.

Couldn't breathe.

Couldn't think.

I could only lie on top of the shade's withered, desiccated body as my vampire healing slowly put me back together.

Finally, when my muscles and bones stopped screaming, I sat up. The shade's dagger had pierced its chest, the impact so hard it'd crushed the entire sternum. I shivered, crawling away from the dead body and lurching to my feet.

Footsteps pounded on the stone steps, and a moment later, Sol, Jerrett, and Malcolm stood in the entrance to the room.

The knot in my chest loosened at the sight of them. Jerrett's shirt was stained with blood, and the earthy, smoky scent of it made my mouth water. But the wound appeared to be healing over already.

"Are you okay?" I gasped. "Was that the last shade?"

I moved toward them, but stopped suddenly when I caught sight of their stony faces.

Shit. They were pissed. And they had a right to be—I'd disobeyed Malcolm and barely survived my reckless maneuver.

"I'm sorry. I know I should've followed your orders, Malcolm. But I didn't see another way."

They didn't respond, just kept staring at me.

"I didn't mean to go over the ledge with that guy! I wouldn't have done it on purpose. I'm not crazy."

That got no response either. Worry began to creep up my spine. I'd seen these men trade banter while fighting dangerous, undead supernaturals. What could possibly be so bad it rendered them speechless?

Finally, Jerrett opened his mouth, his blue eyes shining like pale stars in the darkness.

"No. You're not crazy, Will. You're fae."

29

WILLOW

My brows furrowed as I looked from one brother to another. Neither Sol nor Malcolm laughed at Jerrett's bizarre statement. They looked as serious as he did. More so, maybe.

So I laughed for them, though the sharp huff of air made my still healing ribs twinge with pain.

"What are you talking about? You mean fae, as in fairy? No, I'm a vampire."

The last word came out with surprising ease. Maybe I was finally getting used to the idea, used to my new life.

And now they were trying to tell me that wasn't true?

"I was human, then I became a vampire. You turned me."

I spoke slowly, as if maybe they'd forgotten that night and needed a gentle reminder.

Sol stepped toward me as his mouth dropped open slightly. He cupped my cheek, running a few loose strands of hair through his fingers. Goose bumps rose on my skin at his touch. At the look in his eyes.

"It's true, Willow. I've always smelled it on you. I didn't

recognize the scent for what it was because it's been so many years since I've smelled it. I thought the fae were gone. All but extinct. But you have fae blood. I'm sure of it."

Malcolm and Jerrett came closer. Their expressions matched Sol's—a confusing mixture of fierce hunger, shock, and worry.

"You were never human. Not fully anyway." Malcolm's strong brows pulled together. "You've been part fae your entire life. Yes, you are a vampire now, but not only that. You're a vampire-fae hybrid."

I had no idea what that meant. The word "fae" made me think of little pink-winged fairies flitting around throwing sparkly dust on things. I'd never done anything even remotely like that in my life. And I definitely didn't have wings. I would've noticed.

But Malcolm didn't say the word like he was talking about something cute and pretty. The way he said it made them seem dangerous.

Were these fae creatures worse than vampires? And how could I have spent my whole life as one and not even known it?

I stepped away from Sol's touch, licking my lips. "How do you know? What makes you so sure all of a sudden? You never told me I was fae before. Why now?"

Jerrett snorted. "Because you just went incorporeal on us, sweetheart. And you have Sight. That's fae."

"But you knew about the Sight before! And the shades can go incorporeal. I'm not the only one!" I sounded defensive, and I wasn't sure why. Probably because I was sick of having the rug pulled out from under me every time I thought I'd gotten my bearings.

"Sure they can, Will. But lots of undead creatures can do that. It's kind of a hallmark of their kind." Jerrett flashed a smile, but he was still staring at me ravenously.

"He's right," Sol murmured. "The only living supernaturals who are able to phase in and out like that are fae. Not all of them can do it, but no other species is able to at all."

I thought about that for a second, trying to find a weak spot in his argument. But how could I? Everything I knew about supernaturals, I'd learned from them. I couldn't argue that some other supernatural being possessed this power—I didn't even know what other kinds of magical creatures existed.

"All right. Fine." I chewed on my lip, trying to keep my unease at bay. "So I'm fae. What does that mean, exactly? Why are you all staring at me like that?"

The brothers shared a look, but no one spoke. My stomach dropped precipitously.

"No! No way! You can't do that. You can't drop something like this on me and then not tell me what it means." I smacked Sol's chest, hard.

He trapped my hands against the firm muscles of his pecs, his fingers curling around mine as his thumbs caressed my skin. I didn't want to let it, but the contact soothed me. The blond vampire stepped forward, closing the gap between us and inhaling my scent. I felt his whole body shudder as he breathed in, tensing under my touch.

"It means you're in much more danger than we ever knew, Willow tree."

Worry cascaded through me. Sol wasn't prone to hyperbole or overreaction, so if he said I was in danger, I most definitely was.

"From who? The shades?"

"Yes. But not just them. There are other creatures who would come after you if they knew you were fae. Those who are responsible for nearly wiping the fae out in the first place."

I swallowed, my fingers curling into his soft, dark shirt. "What kinds of creatures?"

"Vampires."

My heart stopped.

I tugged my hands away from Sol's grip, stepping back quickly, but Jerrett caught me in his arms.

"Not from us, sweetheart. Never from us," he murmured softly in my ear, his breath stirring my hair. "And even *we* couldn't smell it strongly enough on you to be sure until now. No one else ever needs to know."

He was right. I'd been living with them for the past week and a half, and despite how close we'd gotten, none of them had ever realized there was anything off about me. Besides, they'd told me they were lone hunters by choice. Maybe I would never even have to meet another vampire. As curious as I'd been to encounter others of our kind, I'd been nervous about it too—and this just gave me one more reason to avoid it.

That still didn't answer the question of what I was though. What were fae?

I twisted, looking up into Jerrett's angular face. "So, what does this mean? I don't feel any different. I never had magic powers growing up or—"

A plaintive cry pierced the still air of the church, and my stomach dropped.

Oh shit. The kids!

I'd been so distracted fighting for my life and then processing this strange new revelation that I'd completely forgotten to check on the little goblin children.

There had been more shades in my vision. Had they arrived at last, the backup to their undead brethren?

"The little ones!"

I raced out of the small room, emerging on one side of the

raised dais where the altar sat.

Bright light pierced my eyes, temporarily blinding me. I stopped, raising a hand to block the beam. The little boy I'd handed the flashlight to stood just outside the door to the office. He swiveled, making the circle of light bounce along a side wall. It took both his little hands to hold the thing, and his grip on it seemed tenuous.

I dashed down the stairs, past several shriveled corpses of shades, and scooped the goblin boy up in my arms before pushing into the office. The other kids were still huddled in the nook created by the desk and the filing cabinet.

"Oh, thank God," I breathed. Then I amended my words. "Thank Fate."

I wasn't sure anymore if God existed. Maybe he was just another supernatural being I had yet to learn about. Regardless, the one who seemed to be listening to my prayers lately was Fate.

The little boy pointed the flashlight up at the ceiling, and when I turned back toward the brothers as they entered the room, the light caught the underside of my face. I was sure I looked ghoulish, like someone telling a scary story around a campfire.

Was that what they would think of me now? That I was some kind of monster? They'd looked both frightened and hungry when they learned I was fae. Why?

I wanted to press them for more answers, but my brain rebelled. There would be time enough for that later. Right now, I needed to focus on what had brought us here. Saving these kids.

As if he'd read my thoughts, Malcolm stepped forward. In a surprisingly gentle gesture for such a large warrior, he tugged the flashlight out of the boy's hand, chucking him under the chin. "I'll take that, little man."

"We need to get them out of here," I said, meeting his gaze over the boy's head.

"We do." Malcolm set the flashlight on a bookcase, allowing it to light the room as a makeshift lamp. "But it's too late to head back tonight. The sun will be up in an hour or so."

I wondered if that was some sense vampires developed over time. I certainly hadn't yet. I'd have to work on paying more attention to the clock so I didn't end up getting trapped outside somewhere and burning to a crisp.

"So what do we do?" I hitched the boy higher on my hip, looking over at the huddle of other kids.

"We wait until tomorrow night. We can seal off this room so no light gets in, and it should be safe until then."

"Safe? Are you kidding me? What if more of those shades show up?" I tried to keep the panic out of my voice, but I felt the boy shudder in my arms. I rocked him gently, swaying my hips back and forth as I spoke in a quieter, calmer voice. "We'd be sitting ducks."

"I know." Malcolm pursed his lips. "It's not ideal. But I highly doubt the shades will return during the day. They can walk in daylight, but most creatures of darkness choose not to. The sunlight weakens them."

I glanced down at the goblin boy cradled in my arms. We didn't really have a choice. We'd never make it back across the border before the sun rose, and these kids were safer here with us than they would be wandering on their own through the woods.

"Okay. We'll stay here."

Almost as if they'd been waiting for my go-ahead, Sol and Jerrett stepped out of the room, returning a few moments later with the long, padded seat of a pew. They propped it against the wall, blocking part of the small window, then repeated the process with a second large plank, masking the window entirely.

They shoved the desk a few feet to the left to brace the pieces of wood, making sure not to step on the huddled kids as they did. Then Jerrett pulled his shirt over his head, and Sol did the same. I tried not to drool as the ambient glow from the flashlight illuminated their carved, muscled torsos.

"Why are we getting naked?" The question was meant to sound casual, but the hitch in my voice gave me away.

Jerrett shot me a smile that practically curled my toes. I wanted to lick all the blood off his lean stomach, and I didn't even care how disgusting that would've sounded to my past self.

"We aren't getting naked, sweetheart. Unless you want to." He winked. "We just need something to keep the light out. Come on, Mal, cough up."

Grimacing, Malcolm tugged his shirt over his head too, tossing it to Jerrett. He and Sol worked quickly, stuffing the fabric into any cracks around the window where sunlight might shine through.

While they worked, I set the little goblin kid down, and he rejoined the pile of his friends. I wished I could talk to them and explain what was going on. Ask their names.

But from the way the little boy had clung to me, they knew by now that we were here to help. They trusted us. That would have to be enough.

"There!" Jerrett hopped down from the desk, dusting off his hands in satisfaction. "That'll do for a day."

A bone-deep exhaustion suddenly settled over me. Everything had happened so fast since we arrived that I'd hardly had time to process any of it.

Jesus. Less than an hour ago, I'd fallen from a three-story bell tower locked in an embrace with an undead creature. And now I stood in a tiny, dark room with seven goblin children and three shirtless vampire men.

What the hell is my life?

But that thought didn't have the same sting it once had. *This* was my life, and as unnerving and terrifying as it sometimes was—as many new questions as I now had—I wouldn't have traded it for anything.

These kids would see their families again because of us. Humans didn't even know they existed. The vampire king apparently didn't care enough to intervene. No one else would've come for them if we hadn't.

There were dark things in the world. I'd known that long before I became a vampire.

But not all dark things were evil. Some of them kept the evil at bay.

I settled onto the floor a few feet away from the mass of little gray-brown bodies. The pile of limbs was starting to slowly unwind as the frightened children peeked up and blinked at us. Sol surprised me when he gently scooted me forward and sat down between me and the wall, pulling me into the cradle of his body.

"Sleep, Willow tree. We'll keep watch."

We had time—all day, in fact. We could talk more. I had so many questions. But his voice was like a sedative, and my body responded almost instantly. I felt Malcolm's large hand rest on my knee, and Jerrett dropped a kiss to my cheek.

"Our little fae. We'll never let you go."

I wasn't sure if I imagined those whispered words, or if I actually heard them.

But before I could decide, sleep took me.

30

WILLOW

I DREAMT OF THREE MEN.

One had eyes like ice—clear blue and crystalline, but warmer than ice could ever be. One had golden skin and wavy, shining hair, and his unseeing gaze penetrated my very soul. One had secrets and pain buried in his dark eyes, and a massive, muscular frame that made me feel small and fragile.

I dreamt of their blood. It dripped from small puncture wounds in their necks, wounds I somehow knew *I* had made. The deep red ribbons of blood cascaded down their bodies, trailing across the ridges of their muscles.

They were shirtless again. I feasted on the sight as a scorching heat rose in my core, my clit throbbing with need. My gaze drifted downward, and my breath caught. I'd been wrong. They weren't just shirtless. They were completely naked.

Three thick, hard cocks stood at attention, the veins on the velvety skin pulsing as they pointed toward me, as if seeking out my wet heat even through the space that separated us.

My hands roamed over my body, massaging my aching

breasts and peaked nipples, trying to quench the fire burning inside me. I glanced down, the men's hot stares still devouring me, and was surprised to see I wore a dress. It was simple in design, but stunning. Gold fabric clung lightly to the curves of my body, shimmering like liquid metal.

Two thin straps rested over my shoulders, and without a thought, I slipped them off. The dress, beautiful as it may be, was nothing but an impediment right now. As the fabric pooled at my feet, three low growls met my ears, the sound filling me with such sharp need that I squeezed my thighs together.

"No, sweetheart. You don't get to hide away like that. Open for us."

Jerrett stepped forward, sliding his hand down my stomach and lightly brushing my clit before slipping one thick finger inside me. I gasped, spreading my legs wider even as my inner muscles clamped down around the intrusion. His icy gaze burned as he nipped my lower lip with sharp teeth, licking away the spot of blood that welled.

He stepped out of the way, withdrawing his finger and trailing my wetness across my skin as Sol dropped to his knees in front of me. He devoured me, lapping at my clit with the flat of his tongue before strumming it in quick, hard strokes. My knees buckled. Jerrett caught me from behind, his cock pressing between my ass cheeks as he palmed my breasts with hot hands.

My pleasure began to peak, and I drove my fingers into Sol's golden hair as Jerrett held me up, grinding into me from behind.

Just as the wave crested, I met Malcolm's eyes. Unlike his brothers, he still stood at a distance from me, his face hard and his gaze locked on mine. He fisted his cock, dragging his hand up and down in rough, angry pulls. Misery and ecstasy washed over his features as he watched me come, a roar belting from his lips as he followed close behind me.

White light flooded my vision.

A voice whispered in my ear.

"You're ours, little fae. And we will never let you go."

I JERKED AWAKE, aftershocks of a powerful orgasm cascading through my body.

Gasping, I looked up… straight into Jerrett's sinfully smirking face. I had somehow ended up sprawled across all three men's laps as I slept, and I was positive they could smell the evidence of my arousal.

Hell, I could smell it.

"Good dream? What was it about, Will?" Jerrett tugged his lip ring into his mouth, watching me intently.

"You," I murmured, blinking in the darkness.

I rolled over onto my other side so I could look up at them without craning my neck. Jerrett cradled my head in his lap, Sol supported my middle, and Malcolm held my legs.

Jerrett's pierced eyebrow shot up. "Yeah? Which one of us?"

"All of you."

The words escaped my lips without thought, but for once, I felt no shame or embarrassment. Something had shifted in me while I slept, a change that had been coming on for days. Like a snake shedding the last of its old skin, I wriggled my body, stretching luxuriously on their warm laps and reveling in the feel of the steely thighs beneath me.

Jerrett's gaze instantly grew heated, Sol smiled with

satisfaction, and just like in my dream, Malcolm's jaw ticked, his face stony.

I wasn't sure what his problem was, but I didn't let it bring down the high I was still floating on from my dream. I gazed up at the three men who had, in such a short time, come to mean more to me than my husband of nine years.

"Thank you." I let my gaze settle on Malcolm, making sure he saw the truth in my eyes as I spoke. "I don't know if I ever said that, but thank you. For saving my life. I'm so glad you did."

Malcolm nodded, his eyes still stormy, but his expression softening slightly. "You're welcome, wildcat."

"I know Fate meant for us to find you." Sol rested his large hands on my waist.

My nipples, already peaked and aching from my dream, stiffened again at his touch, and I wriggled.

"Fuuuck." Jerrett gave a tortured moan. He shook his head, shoving back the dark hair that fell over his eyes. "We gotta get the fuck out of here. There are kids here, and I'm about to... Damn it! Sweetheart, remember this moment. When we get home, I want to hear *all* about that dream." He shook his head, sucking a breath through his teeth. "In. Fucking. Detail."

With another groan, he gently lifted my head so he could stand, adjusting the sizable bulge in his pants as he did. I stared at it, suddenly as desperate as he was to get back to their house.

But he was right. We had a job to finish first. Helpless kids were counting on us.

Malcolm tapped my feet, and I sat up, perching on Sol's lap for a moment as the large, dark-haired man rose. Sol inhaled deeply, drawing in my scent, then he and I stood too.

"What time is it?" I asked, stretching again. The goblin children, recovering from their terror, had spread out around the room. Some still slept, while others whispered to each other in a guttural language I couldn't understand.

"Just after sundown. We need to leave soon. We were about to wake you when you… woke yourself." Malcolm looked away and nodded to Jerrett. "We need to do a sweep of the building before we leave. See if we can find any clues that might lead us to the shades' master. And we should bring a body back with us. Sol, find the most intact one you can. It'll give us a chance to study the full rune pattern."

"What should I do?" I called, as the three of them headed for the door.

"Watch the little ones."

Then they were gone, leaving me to babysit a septet of goblin children.

Part of me was offended, although another part of me acknowledged Malcolm just wanted to keep me safe. And in a way, leaving me alone with the kids demonstrated his faith in me. If he was truly an overprotective, controlling jerk, he would've made me trail after him like some kind of pet just so he could keep an eye on me.

I gathered up the kids, eyeing their bony arms and thin faces with worry. When was the last time they'd eaten? We hadn't brought any food with us. An oversight, maybe, although I had no idea what goblins ate.

Herding seven increasingly rambunctious kids who didn't understand a word I said proved to be a challenge. I finally stole an idea from the preschool groups I'd seen in my old neighborhood and tied the men's shirts together into a makeshift rope. I showed each of the kids how to hold onto it, making it into a game. Once they were all attached to the line, I led them from the room, a chorus of whispered goblin babble following behind me.

The soft glow of twilight still hung in the air, and the interior of the church was brighter than it'd been in the dead of night. There was less left to the imagination, but that wasn't necessarily a good thing. The bloodstained altar stood out like an evil mark on this once worshipful place. I wanted to inspect it more closely, but I didn't dare bring the kids near it. The things they must've seen...

I shoved the thought down, refusing to dwell too long on the ones we hadn't been able to save. We'd done what we could. Next time, we'd do better. Mainly by trying to make sure there *was* no next time.

The pale faces of the women in the woods sprang to my mind suddenly.

They must have something to do with the shades. There was no other reason for them to be here. But why did they vanish? Why not stay and fight?

A noise outside the church caught my attention. The faint rustle of movement in the grass. I tensed.

Had those eerie women returned?

I tugged on the rope, pulling the children into an empty row of pews midway up the aisle.

"Stay here. Get down." I demonstrated, and they followed my lead, staring up at me with wide eyes.

Jerrett and Malcolm had headed up to the tower. I didn't know where Sol was.

"Sol?" I whispered into the gloom.

No answer came, but the door creaked open.

I darted forward to pick up a makeshift weapon from the

floor, but before I fully straightened, several figures walked into the church.

They weren't shades. Nor were they the pale women.

The man in front was large, almost as big as Malcolm. He wore a cape with a fur neckline, a finely tailored shirt and pants, and heavy boots that somehow made no sound on the old church floor. Six other people stood behind him, arranging themselves like ripples in his wake, spreading out and flanking him.

"Hello." The newcomer's voice was deep and smooth. "What have we here?"

I opened my mouth then closed it again, unsure what to say. I'd been prepared to fight, and that impulse still hovered beneath the surface of my skin. But I didn't know quite what to do with his polite formality.

"Who are you?" I blurted.

He cocked his head, studying me. "Carrick Gael. The vampire king of North America. Who are *you*?"

My jaw went slack. This was the vampire king?

I barely registered myself saying, "Willow Tate."

"Willow Tate." He chewed on the words, narrowing his eyes. "Well, Willow. I'm going to assume you're not the one who's been abducting supernaturals. Correct me if I'm wrong, and we'll very happily kill you. But you don't strike me as the type."

"No. No, it wasn't me." I licked my lips. He'd spoken casually, but nothing about his demeanor made me think he was joking.

"Good. Then do you know who did this?"

"Shades."

Malcolm's booming voice behind me made me jump, slamming my heart rate into high gear.

He strode quickly down the aisle past me, the withered corpse of one of the shadow creatures slung across his shoulders. When he reached the man—the *king*—he stopped, hefted the shade over his head, and dropped it at the king's feet.

It hit the floor with a dull thud.

The king stared down at it for a moment, then looked back up at Malcolm. Sol and Jerrett had entered with him and now stood protectively in front of me, the muscles of their bare backs flexing with tension.

"I see." Carrick pursed his lips. "So the shades were the ones attacking supernaturals. And may I ask why *you* are here?"

"Because this threat is about more than just shades. Someone stands behind them, guiding them for some purpose. They're a threat to humans and supernaturals, and we came to stop them from killing innocents."

Carrick's long, broad face split in a sardonic smile. "How noble of you."

Malcolm grimaced. "Someone has to do it… father."

He paused before forcing out the last word, and my mouth fell open.

31

MALCOLM

My father smirked, seeming amused by my response. I could almost hear the thoughts churning in his mind though. He didn't like that I'd stolen his grand gesture—didn't like showing up late to a battle that had already been fought and won.

Too fucking bad, old man. Do your job next time, and maybe you won't miss out on the glory.

It was technically his duty to protect the North American territories from threats like this, but he hadn't taken that duty seriously in hundreds of years, if he ever had. Why he'd decided to show up and play rescuer this time, I had no idea. Unless the shade attacks had spread so far and wide that unrest and fear had forced him into action.

That seemed the most likely possibility. Thomas, our werewolf informant, had told us the attacks had been going on much longer than we'd suspected. People must be getting anxious. I'd never known my father to act unless he was backed into a corner.

"Well," he said, his voice booming with false joviality, "as you can see, your intervention wasn't needed. We would've dealt with these creatures ourselves quickly enough. It's a pity, really. My hunters have been tracking them for several weeks, and I promised them a good fight." His eyes glittered with malice, though his smile didn't falter. "But then again, if our paths hadn't crossed, I never would've gotten to meet your charming new friend, Willow."

His gaze shifted over my shoulder, and my blood turned to ice. I could feel my brothers closing ranks behind me, trying to shield the wildcat from my father's searching gaze. But it was no use. They knew him as well as I did, and we all knew he wouldn't let this go.

"Willow… what did you say your last name was, my dear?" The old bastard cocked his head.

Behind me, Willow cleared her throat. I could hear her heart pounding in her chest as she stepped up lightly beside me. "Willow Tate."

"That was it." The face so much like my own it sickened me smiled beatifically at the girl. "Tell me, my child. What are you?"

Her eyelashes fluttered as her gaze shot quickly to me. Asking a wordless question, searching for guidance on what to tell him.

Damn it, little wildcat, I wish I knew.

She couldn't admit she was fae. That was out of the question. And she couldn't claim to be human either. Her blood smelled too strongly of the supernatural for that. There was no *good* option, only a lie of omission that delayed inevitable disaster.

I rested my hand on the small of her back possessively, feeling her body relax slightly under my touch.

"She's a vampire."

A smile spread across Carrick's face like dawn breaking—slow, and just as deadly as the rising sun. "Is she now? Well, it is truly lovely to make your acquaintance, my dear. I thought I knew all the vampires in the North American territories."

I heard the implicit threat in his words, but Willow didn't know the danger she was in. She took Carrick's offered hand, greeting the viper with polite confusion.

Goddamnit. This is all my fault. This *is why we should have let her go.*

Anger and regret burned in my veins. I'd known this day might come from the moment we'd turned her, had felt it hanging over us all like the threat of a storm.

Perhaps we should have let her die on the street that night. Perhaps it would've spared her greater suffering.

But even as the thought passed through my head, my body and soul rebelled against it. No. That truly hadn't been an option. There'd been something about her even then that had made it impossible to walk away. And now that I knew what she was? Now that I knew *her,* the goodness and strength of her soul? It was unfathomable.

We couldn't fight my father. Not with the guards he had backing him, and the dozens more likely waiting outside. The king was smart enough and cowardly enough not to step into a battle unless he was sure he could win.

It would be foolish to take him on.

Still, when he spoke again, I was sorely tempted to try.

"Malcolm, you must bring your new friend to the Penumbra. Sol and Jerrett too. It's been far too long since you've been home."

The hand splayed across Willow's back tightened into a fist, curling around a handful of her shirt. She looked up at me, worry in her eyes.

For her sake, I forced my muscles to unbunch and called a

stiff smile to my face. "Of course, father. Thank you for the kind invitation. We'd be delighted."

"What about the children?" Willow interjected.

"The *children*?" Carrick's eyebrows shot up.

"The goblin children. The ones the shades kidnapped. They need to be returned to their families. Isn't that why you came here?"

My wildcat looked Carrick right in the eye, her spine straight and head held high, and warmth filled my chest. My father, whatever else he might be, was very charming—but Willow had seen through his charismatic facade immediately.

Ire flashed in his dark eyes at being called out by a fledgling vampire, but Carrick nodded smoothly. "Of course, my dear. My guards will see them home safely. You needn't worry."

That, at least, was true. He *would* return the children unharmed. Goblins were a generally peaceful, reclusive race... and their blood tasted like wet mulch. These young ones had nothing to fear from Carrick's vampire guards.

Unfortunately, it meant we had no excuse not to return to the Penumbra with Carrick right now. And he knew that, judging by the satisfied smirk that crawled across his face.

He gestured with two fingers, and four of the men behind him stepped forward, gathering up the children. Then Carrick turned on his heel, leaving us no choice but to follow.

I pushed gently on Willow's back, urging her forward. Jerrett and Sol fell into step close behind us as the remaining two guards gathered up the shade's broken body.

My wildcat didn't protest, but I could feel her stealing glances at me as we walked. I kept my face impassive and my gaze trained straight ahead, hiding my churning thoughts behind a blank mask.

Defeat weighed like an anchor on my soul. It wasn't an emotion I was used to, and I didn't like it.

We had come here to destroy the shades and free the children, and we'd at least succeeded in that. But the person controlling those undead creatures was still out there, and by now they must know someone was trying to stop them.

What was worse, Carrick's arrival had thrust Willow into a more dangerous world than she was prepared for. A world I'd tried and failed to keep her away from.

We had never declared her, had hoped to keep her existence a secret from the king, but now it was too late to hide her away.

And if my father found out what she truly was, she would be doomed.

I'm sorry, wildcat. I'm so sorry. I hope you live to forgive me.

~

THANK YOU FOR READING!

I hope you enjoyed reading *Saved by Blood* as much as I loved writing it. And don't worry, there's more coming!

There will be more intrigue, badassery, and steam in book two, *Seduced by Blood.*

Can the men who turned Willow keep her safe from their own kind? And can they protect her from themselves?

One-click on Amazon or read for free in Kindle Unlimited.

If you're hungry for more, you can dive into my completed

reverse harem urban fantasy, *Magic Awakened,* starting with the free prequel novella, *Kissed by Shadows.*

Join my mailing list at https://www.sadiemossauthor.com/subscribe and I'll send you your FREE copy of *Kissed by Shadows*!

MESSAGE TO THE READER

Please consider leaving a review! Honest reviews help indie authors like me connect with awesome readers like you. It is truly one of the best ways you can help support an author whose work you enjoy!

If you liked this book, I would be forever grateful if you'd take a minute to leave a review (it can be as short or long as you like) on my book's Amazon page.

Thank you so much!

ACKNOWLEDGMENTS

First and foremost, thank you to my incredible husband and my sweet puppy for putting up with all my mad ramblings about the worlds and characters in my head.

Thank you, Jacqueline Sweet, for the amazing cover! You really brought Willow to life.

To my amazing beta readers: thank you, thank you, thank you!

ABOUT THE AUTHOR

Sadie Moss is obsessed with books, craft beer, and the supernatural. She has often been accused of living in a world of her own imagination, so she decided to put those worlds into books.

When Sadie isn't working on her next novel, she loves spending time with her adorable puppy, binge-watching comedies on Hulu, and hanging out with her family.

She loves to hear from her readers, so feel free to say hello at sadiemoss.author@gmail.com.

And if you want to keep up with her latest news and happenings, you can join her Facebook group, or follow her on Twitter, Goodreads, and Amazon.

Made in the USA
Lexington, KY
03 January 2019